Ж

ISBN: 978-0-9717351-8-7

Second printing 2009
First published 2005

I M Publishing
Published by I M Publishing
P.O. Box F-40303
Freeport, Grand Bahama Island

e-mail: info@sandinmyshoes.net

Book design: Scott Deal,
Archipelago Design Group

Printed in the United States of America

www.sandinmyshoes.net

Sand In My Shoes...

A Collection of Island Stories

MARINA GOTTLIEB SARLES

IM PUBLISHING
GRAND BAHAMA

To Mummy & Doc

Foreword

It is a delight to provide a Foreword to Marina Gottlieb Sarles' insightful collection of 'snippets of life' painted through the eyes of a child who grew to adulthood influenced by the traditions and lifestyle of remote Bahamian Island settlements far from the sophisticated and developed world from which her German parents escaped. Marina's collection is an important addition to the growing body of Bahamian literature spawned by our growing awareness of ourselves as a people with our own identity —a whole made up of many different but congealing parts.

Her memories of her parents—of a strong no-nonsense mother with a mischievous sense of humour, a loving, gentle and spiritual inner core, and a scientific father whose greatest pleasures came from healing—whether ailing humans or broken animals—allowed her to touch on a spiritual side of life, and to relay to her readers a mystical world in which a connection with the afterlife, or conversing with animals, is as normal as breathing.

Marina's love of her homeland and of the many characters that populated her life is brilliantly displayed through warm recollections of her special relationship with Bahamian housekeepers, cooks and surrogate mothers.

A descendant of a world created by Hitler's racial and cultural hatred against Jews and other minorities in pre-World War II Germany, Marina is able to lay bare for Bahamian evaluation the dangers inherent in racial and ethnic discrimination as expressed by ordinary Bahamians against Haitian immigrants, a difficult but necessary reflection for Bahamians of all walks of life.

Rt. Hon. Hubert A. Ingraham
Prime Minister
Commonwealth of The Bahamas
Member of Parliament
Justice of the Peace

Acknowledgements

I wish to extend my deepest gratitude to those hearts, minds and talents that have helped make this book a reality.

Rt. Hon. Hubert A. Ingraham, Prime Minister of my beloved Bahamas, was so generous to take time out of his extremely busy life to read *Sand in My Shoes*. The Foreword you have written is eloquent, heartfelt and deeply touching. I am honoured. Thank you so much for your indefatigable spirit!

Lady Anne Hampson has been my mentor and my guiding light. A trusted friend, she always told me the truth and never tired of sharing her extensive knowledge of the English language. Thank you, Anne. Love you a million!

Paula Boyd Farrington is a woman whose creative vision is boundless! Her keen aesthetic eye and amazing heart are the magical instruments that orchestrated every page and every chapter. Paula, my dearest friend, I am in awe of you! I simply cannot thank you enough.

Christine Matthäi and Shawnie Dickie are the two sisters who showed up much later in my life. Christine's perceptive and thoughtful eye helped choose the cover photograph, while Shawnie edited my sentences with the heart of an angel. Thank you both for believing in me and sharing your feminine wisdom.

Elly Decter diligently proofread and edited the pages, placing the many needed commas without ever making me feel that I should take a punctuation class! Elly, I feel blessed beyond words that you shared your time and took on this project. Thank you so much!

Scott Deal at Archipelago Design Group is the creative magician who captured the essence of *Sand in My Shoes* in his brilliant graphic design. Moreover, he was patient beyond words. Thank you Scottie, my fellow Bahamian, for putting all the pieces together!

Sally Lightbourn is a precious friend whose eagle eyes searched the final, final copy. Sally, you are The Queen of Proper British Spelling and em—dashes (yes, I know that should be a hyphen!) Thank you for your time and wonderful support.

My friends of the Creative Writer's Circle were the ones who listened to my stories and never tired of nudging me on. In our sacred communion, I grew to have faith in my own work. Thank you.

Jamie Sarles, my husband, made it all possible and encouraged me to trust myself. The support and love he so generously shares have given my heart wings to follow its greatest longing. Thank you Jamie, forever.

Nikolai, my son, listened with the honest ears of a child. He is the one who helped me discover the title *Sand in My Shoes*. Thank you Nikolai, for the times you gave up basketball to sit with me and listen.

My father, Dr Ejnar F. Gottlieb, and my mother, Owanta Gottlieb von Sanden, were amazing storytellers. Whatever I learned in this regard, I learned from them. I kiss you both. I know someday we will sit together once more, at a round table in the sky.

Prologue

When I started writing this collection of Bahamian vignettes, I was worried that the book held no theme. How can anyone just write snippets of life? Snapshots never tell the entire story.

However, the stories seemed to touch those who read them and so I began to think that if a story can produce a smile or a fleeting teardrop, then it may have some meaning.

These stories are not my memoirs by any means. They are simply a few of the inspirational threads that have been woven into the life of an island girl, who happens to be the daughter of German immigrants.

After searching for a strong connecting theme, I realized that it is the sacred in all things which binds us. We are connected through laughter, just as we are united when tragedy strikes; a movement occurs in our souls bringing us into communion with each other and with the greater Mystery.

As a child, I searched for some sort of meaning to life. I am eternally grateful to these Bahamian isles, especially Abaco and Grand Bahama, for here, among extraordinary people and multi-faceted prisms of light and colour, my spirit was allowed to blossom while being nourished by the rich vein of human experience.

I have wept in caves where emerald green water drips into silence. At the same time, I have felt my heart illuminated with joy while looking straight into the black face of death. For me, the intimacy of island community is the anchor in life's deep ocean, as well as the buoy that lets me float in a sea of wonder.

These stories are a small kaleidoscope of life in The Bahamas. Many of them are true, while others are truth wrapped in myth. As the author, I hope that they find resonance within you.

A Collection of Island Stories

Contents

The Sands of Time...

The Circumstantial Dentist

In the 1940's, Pine Ridge was truly a pioneer settlement. As I grow older and have a greater understanding of life, I am indeed awed by the courage and tenacity it must have taken to live in a place so isolated from civilization. I try to imagine what my parents must have felt when they flew over the flat, desolate island of Grand Bahama, and stepped out of the rocking seaplane into a small dinghy, which carried them to the rickety pier jutting far out into the shallow water. They were educated people, coming from war-torn Germany. Until Hitler's rise to power, they had both lived in luxury. My mother, an aristocrat from East Prussia, held a degree in Zoology, while my father, the son of a wealthy dentist in Dresden, was now to be the first medical doctor on the island. They were foreigners in a strange land, brought here by the hand of fate, and a wealthy American businessman named Wallace Groves.

Mr Groves had acquired the rights to cut down the yellow pines on Grand Bahama Island. Some eight hundred lumber-jacks worked for his company. My father's job was to give

medical attention to those injured by the cruel blade of a power-saw, as well as others in the settlement who were just downright sick or diseased. Living conditions were so primitive that no American doctor wanted the position. Their life was devoid of comfort. Grocery stores were non-existent; food was scraped from cans until my mother could harvest fresh vegetables from her own garden and my father learned how to catch fish in the sea. Their home was a hut built close to a sawmill and a high smoking chimney. The air was often heavy with dust and flies. Where my mother came from, this new home would have been deemed a pigsty.

But hardship has a way of making or breaking people, and these two immigrants were not going to give up easily. Life was precious to them and, fortunately, they were both blessed with a sense of humour—a gift which was probably their greatest survival tool.

One day, my father was off island buying medical supplies in Nassau. No one liked it when he went away because he was the only doctor. Well, it just so happened that one of the villagers, Mr Rupert, had a toothache. Obviously, he had been struggling with the pain, but finally, at midnight, when he could no longer bear it, he started banging on our front door.

'Nurse Gottlieb,' he said through swollen gums, 'you gotta pull my tooth 'cause I just can't live another minute like this.'

'Rupert,' my concerned mother replied, 'I'm not a dentist. I've never pulled a tooth before!'

'Well, Nurse, I'm willing to be the first person you practice on, 'cause I may as well die if this pain don't stop.'

And so, wearing just pajamas and flip-flops, she steered Rupert past the outdoor movie theater, towards what the locals called the clinic.

The clinic in Pine Ridge was just a wooden shack resembling a chicken coop, yet my father performed amazing surgical feats in that tiny office, from delicate eye operations to basic hemorrhoidectomies.

Now, it was my mother's turn to prove herself. She must have been terrified at the thought of attempting such a procedure. But pioneers are often forced to rely on their own resourcefulness, and she was no exception. Setting up the sterile table, she laid out the pliers and the syringe filled with novocaine. Her fingers were sweating as the needle found its mark and she pumped the numbing substance into Rupert's sore gum.

'Well Rupert,' she said, quietly praying that the nerve was dead, 'Doc always waits for about ten minutes, so sit back and relax.'

Thankfully, the nerve complied. Mother sat down on the white stool that didn't roll. Rupert watched her pick up the pliers and brace her feet against the floor. She was not a weak woman. God knows, she was built like a German Amazon. Clamping those hard, metal tongs around that wisdom tooth, she started pulling; the only trouble was, the tooth had a mind of its own.

'No wonder they're called wisdom teeth!' she thought, as she pried and pulled. 'They're too smart to let go!'

She tried kneeling to get a better angle; still nothing moved. Sweat began to trickle over her brow. Sensing her frustration, Rupert tried to calm her, but his words just came out in grunts. It's not easy talking with a mouth that's forced open.

Mother was becoming more and more panicky. Rupert knew she was swearing in another language. When she said,

'Verdammt!' in German, he figured the word meant damn

in English and he was sure he recognized other curse words.

After struggling for some time, she yanked the pliers from his mouth and said,

'Rupert, you're going to have to wait until Doc comes home!'

'No! Nurse Gottlieb!' he implored. 'Please don't give up on me just yet. I can't live with the pain when this tooth wakes up.'

So there they were at loggerheads; Mother was totally frustrated and wanted to stop, but Rupert wouldn't let her.

'Rupert,' she exclaimed impatiently, 'if I break the tooth, Doc will kill me!'

Rupert must have looked mighty pitiful because all at once a look of determination crossed my mother's face.

'Ah, to hell with it!' she blurted, 'I'm trying one more thing! Maybe this position will work. Just hold on Rupert!'

With that, she straddled her patient as if she were mounting a horse, and plunked herself right down on his lap, commanding him to throw back his head and open wide once more.

'I'm going to wrench this tooth out if it kills me!' she cried.

So there was my mother sitting on Rupert's lap. Rupert could only imagine what a passerby might think if they looked into the window.

'Lord!' he thought, 'Here is Nurse Gottlieb in her dressing gown, straddling my lap. If anybody sees this, they may get the wrong idea! And oh my Lord! What if they tell Dr Gottlieb? I better not get sick after this, because he might take a big needle to my backside!'

Mother strained and strained until suddenly, they both heard that crunchy sound that happens when a tooth relinquishes its grip on the jawbone. Fortunately, the whole tooth slid out.

My mother was ecstatic. She always possessed a unique

quality that enabled her to laugh like a child. Jumping off Rupert's lap, she waltzed around the room, holding the tooth in the air and admiring its long, curly root.

'Rupert,' she yelled, hopping up and down. 'We did it! The whole tooth came out!'

Bleary-eyed from exhaustion, Rupert grinned lopsidedly and murmured,

'Nurse Gottlieb, now I know why Doc married you. You are quite a woman, and besides, you just made the grade to bein' a dentist on demand!'

The Potcake's Tale

The little mongrel ran out into the road. She had just been playing hide and seek with her friends, crouching behind the tough green ferns that grew so freely in the yellow pine forest. Every so often, they would all sit back on their skinny haunches, eyes riveted on the huge horseflies, waiting until one came close enough. Then, with a loud snap of their jaws, the dogs would bite the air, hoping to catch the hapless victim.

Evening was just falling and the little mongrel noticed her stomach growling. All the frolicking and drooling after horseflies had made her very hungry. She decided to cross the road and make her way to the edge of the Pine Ridge settlement. There, if good fortune were on her side, she might find a garbage can with some leftover scraps of boiled fish and grits. Sometimes she could fill her belly at Mrs Capron's house. Mrs Capron was not particularly fond of dogs, and would not have fed them, but it was her habit to cook huge pots of peas n' rice for her six children. Often the rice at the bottom of her cast-iron pot would cake into a starchy mass, which she would scrape out onto the rocks. This congealed substance

was the staple diet for wild dogs. Although never as tasty as boiled fish, it certainly did the job of stuffing a hungry belly; furthermore, it was this famous dish which gave the Bahamian mongrel the proud name of Potcake.

Tonight, however, there was a problem: she had to hurry because other members of the pack were well acquainted with these take-out meals. Unless she arrived there first, she would go to bed hungry.

So off she ran, her thin body loping across the roughly paved road. Her thoughts were so intent on food that she failed to hear the truck rattling behind her. When she finally noticed the sound of tires bumping over loose gravel, it was too late. She felt a massive blow to her hind leg. The force threw her up into the air, so that she landed in the forest with a loud thump. She squealed helplessly, her ribs moving in and out in a frightened rhythm. The truck did not stop. All she could see were two disappearing tail lights, red buttons fading into the distance.

There was no one to help her. The pain spread through her trembling body. Whimpering, she glanced at her leg. It appeared to have a strange shape, no longer the elegant, slender form she knew, but angled and ungainly. Moving it was excruciating, and so she began to lick the wound, cleaning up the blood that was seeping from a gash between her toes.

At first, she was confused. She lay there taking inventory, as it were, of her body and her state of affairs. Where could she go? People always seemed inclined to kick the wild dogs that lingered around or shoo them away with stones. She groaned at the thought of trying to run. Her leg hurt so badly.

Stars were beginning to twinkle above her; the moon was a red ball hanging over the pine trees, but she remained still.

Her friends must have taken another route because not one came past her, and she felt terribly lonely.

'I have to find help,' she thought, 'or I'll die here.'

Suddenly she remembered the little wooden house at the edge of the village. Every day, she saw people sitting outside on the rickety steps or dozing in the shade of the huge ficus tree.

Many a time she had seen lumbermen carried in on stretchers when their chainsaws had slipped, cutting deeply into their legs or severing their hands. They always went into the shack screaming in pain, but when they came out they wore clean white bandages and seemed to moan far less. The smell of fear had left their bodies.

A tall man worked there. He wore a white uniform, and his kind smile and cheerful words had won the hearts of the villagers. She had heard them say that they were blessed to have a doctor like him.

'Dat man could heal anyting,' they would say. 'In de ol' days we jus' used to lay down and die, but since Doc come, all o' we still livin'. And when it come to diagnosin', dat man so smart. He don't need no fancy machines; he mussee have de second sight, cause he know what wrong wit ev'rybody. And when we ain't got no money, we could still go see him. He ain't never turn nobody away. And he don't get vex when we pay him wid Nassau grouper and crawfish. Lord, we gots to be thankful for dat man!'

The little mongrel dragged herself up, gnashing her teeth in pain. She hobbled on three legs, feeling very faint because of the blood she had lost. Nevertheless she made her way through the woods, hugging the road, until she saw the shack which served as a medical clinic. When she finally arrived at the bottom of the steps, she collapsed, whimpering loudly.

It was late and the doctor was not there, but she could wait. Her body was streaked with sweat and blood; she knew she smelled a bit, but she did not care. If only he would come. She waited patiently all through the night, never taking her eyes off the path that led up to the wooden steps. She longed for the morning, hoping to see his tall figure stride across the rocks and clumps of green crab grass. Her thin body was shivering and she felt thirsty.

The sun rose, warming her gently. She lay there panting, unable to move, so great was the pain. Patients began to arrive, crowding around the tree and sitting on the benches outside. A big man wielding a stick walked towards her.

'Move, you ol' stinky potcake!' he yelled. 'You ain't supposed to be here! Dis clinic ain't for no dogs!'

He raised the stick and was just about to bring it crashing down on her hip, when her attacker's arm was yanked back and a voice roared,

'Jack, if you hit that dog, I will make sure that the next needle I put into your backside is the size of a shark hook!'

Jack's face contorted in fear.

'Oh Doc, I so scared o' dem needles. Please suh, I was jus' tryin' to shoo dis potcake out de way!'

'Well, if you want to make sure that I treat your backside with respect, then give me a hand, and let's carry her onto my operating table. It looks like she's the emergency patient this morning.'

Jack, who was actually terrified of dogs, put on a brave face and slipped a muscular arm under her shoulders. Together they carried the dog into the office. Everyone was curious as to how the treatment would unfold. Children crept up to the door and peered in, whispering and giggling.

'Everybody out!' yelled the doctor. 'She has just as much right to privacy as anyone else!' And the children scampered away, running to hide their faces in their mothers' colourful skirts.

The mongrel's eyes were soft as she looked at the doctor. She tried bravely to wag her tail, but even that small motion sent reams of pain up her spine. She watched as he focused the bright overhead light directly on to her leg.

'It's okay, girl,' he said gently. 'You're a mess, but we'll fix you up. Now listen. Please don't bite me when I give you this needle. I have to sew this gash and then we'll splint your leg. I'll have to pull on it to see if I can straighten it. It will hurt.'

The dog understood the silent pact between them. As she lay there panting, her reflex against the pain set in, and occasionally her body would jerk, but never once did she bare her teeth. As she looked at the man helping her, she was overcome with admiration. His pure love for dogs was so apparent. He worked skillfully, yet he talked with a voice unlike anything she had ever heard. It soothed her like a healing balm. She noticed that his words were spoken in a strange language. Not that she even understood English, but the tone of his voice had changed completely and seemed to have a guttural sound which would swing upwards into a song.

When he was finished, he bent forward and stroking her ear, said,

'Du bist ein braves Maedchen,' which she telepathically guessed to mean 'you're a good girl.'

At that moment, the mongrel fell deeply in love. She would have given her life to stay with the man. Her eyes were filled with gratitude, and she began licking his hands and face. He took a kidney shaped bowl from the shelf and filled it with

cool water, which she lapped greedily. Unwrapping his lunch, he found a tuna fish sandwich, and breaking it into small pieces, he fed her from his own hand. Although she was ravenous, she took the morsels in delicate nibbles, making certain not to nip him. She thought she had died and gone to heaven. The time passed by, yet he did not seem at all perturbed that a crowd was gathering outside. He enjoyed being with her.

However, after chatting with her for some time, he patted her head, lifted her off the table and said,

'I will need to see you tomorrow morning. Please come back.'

He opened the door to his outdoor waiting room, and the little mongrel hobbled down the steps, head held high, as she proudly displayed her white bandages.

The next morning she was there bright and early. She was both surprised and pleased to be treated like royalty. Again, she was his first patient. After removing the bandages over the sutured cut, he carefully cleaned the area with antiseptic. The sharp, clean smell hurt her tender nose, but she did not complain. She was so taken by him that even when he shoved two bitter pills down her throat, she simply swallowed.

'That's to make sure you don't get an infection,' he said. Once again he fed her his sandwich.

For several weeks, the mongrel could be seen waiting for the doctor every morning. As he ambled up the path, his eyes would light up as soon as he caught sight of her. She, in turn, would bark out a greeting and furiously wag her spotted tail, while attempting to extend a front paw.

One day the good doctor said,

'It's time to remove the splint.'

For some reason the mongrel felt a pang of fear. She wondered if that meant she could no longer visit him. As

his smooth hands removed the bandages, which by now had lost their clean white look, she began to whimper. She felt sad, empty. In her doggy world she knew that something was changing and this sent jolts of anxiety to her heart. Never before had she been the recipient of such hospitality and kindness.

He lifted her off the table and said,

'You are fully mended now. You are free to go.'

The little potcake hung her head dejectedly and limped out the door. The doctor watched her leave. Just then Jack entered the ambulatory.

'Doc!' he said with a concerned expression. 'What wrong wid you? You ain't lookin' too good!'

The doctor did not respond but his eyes were cloudy and distant.

'Doc, what happen?' demanded Jack. 'I just come for my high blood pressure pills, but if I is botherin' you, I'll go!'

'No, no,' mumbled the doctor, as he prepared to take Jack's blood pressure, tightening the cuff around the man's arm.

Suddenly he dropped the small rubber ball he was pumping and ran to the door. Yanking it open, he whistled and shouted,

'Amen! Come here, Amen!'

'Lord have mercy!' thought Jack, 'Today sure as hell ain't Sunday! And der ain't no church sermon goin' on. Maybe Doc's workin too hard. I hope he ain't goin' crazy.'

At that moment, the little mongrel came bounding into the office.

Bending down to hug the four legged creature, the doctor asked politely,

'Amen, I was just wondering ... Would you like a new home?'

Joyously consenting, the little mongrel barked loudly.

Jack scratched his head, the rubber tube still dangling from his arm.

'Doc, why on earth you callin' dat potcake 'Amen'?'

'Well, Jack, she's been here every single day, and so I know that I can count on her just like I can count on the amen in church!'

And from that day on, Amen and the good doctor were inseparable.

Miss Blanche

Tension could run very high in our house. My mother was highly strung, and to put it mildly, emotionally volatile. Doors would slam, a few dishes might break, and my father would raise his eyebrows and say,

'Oh! Oh! Mother is on the warpath! Perhaps, we should clear out for a while.'

Usually, I would disappear down to the beach in front of our house and hide in the coconut grove, watching lizards and dragonflies; but occasionally, if I were seated at the dinner table, there would be no escaping the castigation. It was on such an evening that my mother decided to give my life purpose.

She was probably exhausted from bending over all day and delivering babies in shacks just big enough to hold a king-sized bed and a birthing mother.

I was, as many children are, rather snooty about something, and whatever disparaging comment I made was to change the way I viewed the world. I have often wondered if it was that split second in time, which precipitated my future vocation.

I remember exactly what I was eating: homemade chicken

soup. At my remark, my mother got up and came over to me, hauling me up by the collar, while my brothers giggled nervously, relieved that for once they were not the culprits.

'It's time that you develop a social conscience,' she snapped. 'Your life is too easy. You need to see how other people live.'

With that, she dragged me into the kitchen and gave me a quick clout behind the ears. Opening the cupboard, she took out a big bowl, into which she ladled spoonfuls of soup.

'You can forget about your dinner tonight,' she said, covering the bowl with aluminum foil. 'You're going to feed someone who'll be grateful for a meal!'

With that, she dragged me out the front door and down the rocky hill to the house of Miss Blanche. Miss Blanche's dwelling was really a wooden shack in constant need of repair. Whenever we ran past it, the children of the neighbourhood would allude to the fact that a witch lived in that hovel.

'She can't walk no more,' I was told by whispering voices, 'cause she was struck by lightning.'

And now, my mother was telling me that I must go inside and feed the wicked witch. I began to tremble. This was worse than any tongue-lashing or beating my Germanic mother could hand out.

'Don't make me go in there Mummy,' I pleaded. 'She might eat me!'

'Don't be so silly! Miss Blanche is just a poor old woman whose legs are paralyzed.'

I felt sick, and peeked under the aluminum foil covering the bowl to have a look at the chicken leg whose meat had fallen off the bone. I wondered if her legs looked anything like that.

My mother urged me on. I knocked, timidly at first.

'Knock louder!' my mother commanded.

My knuckles rapped on the splintering wood. Suddenly, a tall, scraggly woman with crinkled skin and two missing front teeth pulled the door open. I thought I might faint in fear but, of course, my mother would never have allowed such a thing to happen. She dug her elbow into my ribs.

'Pull yourself together!' she hissed. 'This is Wedny, Miss Blanche's daughter.'

'Why is she called Wedny and not Wendy?' I asked my mother in a hushed whisper.

'I think it's because she was born on a Wednesday,' my mother replied.

I mumbled some sort of greeting while Wedny began to shriek for her sister to come too.

'Geraldine!' she cackled in a high pitched voice. 'Come see Nurse Gottlieb! She done bring her daughter to see us!'

Geraldine appeared from the back room in a soiled cotton skirt, and I quickly assessed that, of the two women, she was perhaps the most practical. Both front teeth were still visible and her yellow brown eyes contained a grain of intelligence. I stepped forward, and was just about to hand her the bowl, when my mother said,

'My daughter has come to spoon feed your mother. Can we go into the bedroom?'

I thought I would die. Go into the old woman's bedroom? I stumbled forward in a trance, expecting any moment to see a bubbling cauldron spouting sulfuric fumes. The air around me reeked of strange, acrid smells. To this day, I can still smell that house somewhere deep in my olfactory system. It was a smell of dust, urine and stale air, all bottled in one room. I felt the urge to throw up, but that would have called forth a worse

fate. Wedny pulled at my sleeve. I looked down at her hand with its cracked red skin and broken fingernails. I cringed, but my mother's presence loomed strong behind me.

I was pushed into a small, dimly lit room, which contained a bed and a rocking chair. Propped against some pillows was the crumpled form of the old woman. The smell of rancid pee assaulted my young nose, and I coughed.

'The longer you are in the presence of that smell, the more you'll get used to it,' my mother said quietly, but ever so firmly. 'It'll fade after a while.'

Then she did an unforgettable thing. Stepping out from behind me, she grasped the faded, white arm of the old woman. Stooping low, she smiled her dazzling Ingrid Bergman smile and kissed the bony, wrinkled forehead. Miss Blanche blinked, and I was astonished to see wisdom and humour hiding in those deeply sunken eyes. She smiled back at my mother, and all I could see was one decaying tooth embedded in the pale gum of her lower jaw.

'This is my daughter,' my mother said. 'She has come to care for you. From now on, she will bring you supper every evening and help feed you.'

Miss Blanche turned her head, straining to see me. Something shifted in me. I am not quite sure how it happened, but suddenly I was no longer afraid. I felt an opening in my heart, a sort of instant connection. Years later, when I became a healer and medical professional, I was able to identify the feeling as compassion. Compassion for humanity, no matter what form it takes, no matter how beauteous or grotesque. Looking at Miss Blanche, I no longer saw an ugly hag, but a person. It was quite miraculous actually. I sat down beside her on that grimy bedspread, and pulling the spoon

from my pocket, I began to ladle the lukewarm liquid into her gaping mouth. She made strange sucking noises as she tried to chew, and when she smacked her thin lips together, her flaccid cheeks would fold inward, making her look even more ancient and misshapen.

My mother left the room. Miss Blanche took her own sweet time to eat her fill. In between mouthfuls, she would close her eyes and lean her head back to relax the muscles of her scrawny neck. At first she said nothing, but I could hear little grunts of pleasure.

When the soup was finished, I said goodbye and she gave me that warm, toothless smile that only the aged can share. Clutching the bowl under my arm, I climbed back up the hill to our house. By now it was dark, and the indigo sky above me twinkled with stars. I felt full even though I had not eaten.

I cannot remember how long I visited Miss Blanche. Children don't seem to take time so seriously. Maybe it was a year, maybe two, I don't know. What comes back to me is that, although I could never entirely yield to the odours in that house, I could still do the task at hand. Years later, when I worked in hospitals as a physical therapist, this ability was very useful. I even remember taking my personal comb to untangle her long matted hair, which felt greasy to my fingers. Dandruff and dirt stuck to her scalp. Her head smelled sour, like decaying tamarinds. I called for Geraldine to bring a big enamel bowl with warm water, and while she prepared it, I ran up to our house for some shampoo. It was that green Clairol Essence shampoo that gave off the fragrance of wild flowers. Together, Geraldine and I lifted Miss Blanche into the rocking chair, and encouraging her to bend over, I washed the old woman's hair. It was not a martyr's act—it was just

something I felt needed doing. I still don't know what unseen force allowed me to do that task. This was also the first time I ever saw her legs. Thin, like the sapless branches of a withered mango tree. Thin poles attached to limp, drooping feet, which dangled helplessly at the ends. Once more the feeling flooded my heart.

One evening, I visited my frail friend. Of late, she was failing more and more. When I entered that musty room, her face seemed to glow incandescent yellow. She turned her head feebly. To my childish eyes she looked like a crushed bird, fallen from a tree.

'Child,' she whispered, 'I know I'm going soon. But Christ Himself is coming to take me home, and I'm happy. His face will shine on mine, and I want you to know that when I see Him, I am going to tell Him that you are a good girl. I will make sure you have a place in heaven. You hear?'

I nodded, not fully registering the meaning of her words.

The next day, when I came to see her, she had passed away. She didn't have a funeral. Certainly her two daughters could never have afforded one, and most likely, no one would have gone, but I felt all the richer for her presence in my life.

Sparky's Bliss

My childhood was undoubtedly touched by people who helped build character, and taught me to look at life from various angles. However, I cannot fail to mention a few of the animals under whose silent tutelage I acquired great insight into the world of nature and life. One of these four-legged instructors was a horse named Sparky. Sparky earned his name because of his firecracker spirit. He was frisky and fresh, kicking up his heels when frolicking was his fancy, and bucking just as stubbornly when the tight girth of his saddle irritated him. My girlish temperament was both enchanted and frightened by his personality. Wrapping my arms around his powerful neck, I would lay my face into the curve of his sleek shoulder, inhaling the horsy smell of him. In those moments, he was my best friend, calm and gentle. However, sometimes when his impetuosity champed at the bit, the snap of a twig or the sound of a mosquito buzzing would make him run like hell, and if I was on his back, my only recourse was to hang on for dear life.

On one of these demon rides, I was thrown to the ground.

It could have been a small hermit crab scuttling under the red hibiscus bush or a mockingbird warbling that freaked Sparky. Anything gave him reason to bolt when he felt like it. The memory of the rocky limestone whizzing past beneath me is framed in my mind. I was chubby, and never as agile as other girls my age, and so I fell hard. The awful snap of wrist bones breaking, fractured the humid air. It was my first experience of real physical pain. Bones are loaded with pain receptors, and mine were no exception. The break was serious, not only because it was a compound fracture, but because the growth cartilage had also been damaged.

My father, normally able to handle any medical emergency, was concerned that my arm might remain deformed, and so he chartered an airplane which flew me to an American hospital. The orthopedic surgeon there was kind, but even he was frustrated when my bones refused to stay in place. It took three attempts. Each time the cast was removed, I could see the surgeon's worried look, but finally the bones healed. The only problem was that inside, I was still unstable and shaking, something the x-ray machine was unable to detect.

My mother, who was a real East Prussian horsewoman, was dead set on me tackling my next hurdle. Never one to coddle or pamper, she set out to teach me true horsemanship.

'You must get over your fear,' she said sternly. 'You have to mount him once more, and show him that you're the boss.'

But I did not feel like the boss. I felt that Sparky had the power, and in my mind, not fully understanding the way horses think, I felt he had breached my trust because of his rash ways. However, there was no arguing with my mother, and so the day came when I was forced to stick my foot into the stirrup and swing myself up onto his back. Feeling small

and vulnerable, I took the reins in my trembling hands, my mother scrutinizing every move.

'Push your heels down! Tighten your knees! Don't jerk his mouth!' she cried.

I knew right then, that I would never ride a horse like my mother. As an equestrian, she possessed an air of elegant confidence that I could only dream about. The horses she had ridden in her youth were bred for a king's stable.

I wanted to shout,

'I hate riding. I'll never be like you! Just leave me alone!'

But Sparky seemed to read my thoughts. For once, he trotted like a show horse in the ring, gallantly picking up his legs and arching his neck in true thoroughbred fashion. Breaking into a gentle canter at my nervous command, he brought his inner leg forward without missing a beat, something I had struggled to teach him in the riding ring for months. He shook his head with solemn dignity as if to say,

'Silly girl, I knew how to do this all along.'

I began to relax and flow with the rhythm of his movements. He seemed serious, as if he were listening to me, soothing my childish concerns with the smooth roll of his powerful muscles, and my fear began to melt like ice in the hot sun.

I swear he knew that, on that day, I needed to pass a test, a test of faith in myself, and he was there to carry me through. I believe he also knew that I had been badly hurt in more ways than one, and that his time for recklessness was over. Together, we needed to work as a team. Being nobody's fool, he sensed my mother's thoughts, realizing that she was the one with the ultimate power, and not above packing him off to the dreary life of a carthorse, if his irrational behaviour became incurable. He was clever. The idea of lifelong confine-

ment would have given him something to ponder. So, without losing his integrity and self-esteem, he conformed in the nick of time—a valuable lesson when others are in charge.

Sparky was a unique character; not only headstrong, but possessing a sense of humour and taste for the good life. He was forever escaping from his corral until, finally, there was no sense in trying to keep him contained. If he didn't push his way through the wooden fence, he jumped it; when we built a higher fence, he simply learned how to lift the bar on the gate. He was a natural born contortionist with freedom on his mind. Needless to say, his jaunts rarely led him to dangerous places. He wasn't interested in running wild in the streets where cars were his competition; no, he was a connoisseur of life. He liked food, liquor and song!

I was introduced to this side of his infamous personality when, walking home one day, I passed Key's Bakery, a tiny shop filled with goodies, just at the bottom of our hill. Bunyan Key was Marsh Harbour's baker, a true legend throughout the cays, but I was afraid of him because he could be gruff and impatient; a characteristic which I now understand, as those in this profession are required to rise long before the dawn. Mr Bunyan had an ophthalmic disorder, which caused one of his lower lids to droop and made the eye water incessantly. I don't know whether this ailment was due to Bell's Palsy or a tumour even, but whatever the cause, I thought his gaze was stern because he never blinked. Whenever I entered the shop to buy a pastry, I would look down and mumble, fearful of looking him straight in the eye. This behaviour must have irritated him and made him think that the doctor's daughter was ill-mannered indeed.

Famous throughout the islands, Mr Bunyan's bread

enticed everyone. Residents from Hopetown, Man-o-War and Guana Cay would travel for miles on Albury's Ferry to hold a loaf of his hot bread in their hands. Children of all ages would gather outside the bakery just for a whiff of his delicious cupcakes, and tourists from all over the world would stuff their suitcases with steaming loaves before leaving Abaco Island. No one could resist a hot fresh loaf from the oven. I remember tearing off huge chunks and stuffing them into my mouth, not caring if my fingers blistered. Some things just smell so good that the smell remains bottled somewhere in your brain. That's how it is with Bunyan's bread. Just thinking about it makes my mouth water.

Apparently, I was not the only one drawn by the smell of delicious bread baking. Walking home that evening, I passed the steps leading up to the bakery. There I saw a big, brown horse's rump, which I immediately recognized as Sparky's. Amazed, I watched as he wedged himself into the narrow porch entrance. Stamping his hoof on the cement floor, he demanded the baker's attention. I stood there in trepidation, not knowing what to do, and expecting Mr Bunyan to explode out of his shop at any minute, yelling furiously for me to remove this rude trespasser. But there was no way that I could squeeze past Sparky's backside and get hold of his head to lead him away. To try pulling his hind legs might have meant getting kicked to kingdom come, so I just watched, paralyzed. Soon, the shop door opened. I cringed, waiting for the angry tempest, but to my surprise, old Mr Bunyan stepped out holding a thick slice of bread, dripping with peanut butter. Smiling kindly, he raised it to Sparky's muzzle, crooning,

'Now, there's a good boy. Do you like my bread?

Everybody likes Mr Bunyan's bread.'

Sparky nibbled away, and when the bread was gone, I thought I saw more water than usual flowing from both Mr Bunyan's eyes.

'Wait, boy,' he whispered. 'I've got something else for you.'

He slipped back into the shop, only to return again with a handful of sugar, which Sparky greedily devoured.

'Come back tomorrow,' Mr Bunyan said, waving farewell, and by damn if Sparky didn't back out of that space as graceful as a swan. Whinnying loudly, he tossed his head as if to say thanks and trotted home. There I was running next to him, contemplating how his direct contact with Mr Bunyan was much more conducive to friendship than my shy mumbling. I realized that even behind a gruff facade, people can be touched by living creatures. I looked at my four-legged friend. A few grains of powdered sugar still sparkled on his soft nose. Sparky had captured Mr Bunyan's heart.

You might think Sparky had been spoiled enough for one day. Not so! He was like an impulsive child, enjoying the moment, looking for adventure, fresh escapades and anything that enhanced the senses. As we crested the hill, notes of Mozart's *Coronation Concerto* floated towards us. My father was home. It was his ritual every evening, after a busy day in the clinic, to sit on the porch overlooking the wide expanse of turquoise water and listen to classical music. We children knew not to disturb this eventide ceremony. It was an unspoken law that we could sit with him, but talking and fidgeting were forbidden, under pain of death.

In his younger days, before studying medicine, my father, Doc, as we affectionately called him, had played the cello with a well-known orchestra led by the famous conductor, Hindemith. Doc's knowledge of music was tremendous, and

it never ceased to surprise me that, not only could he tell you exactly what piece of classical music was playing at any given time, but he recognized who the conductor was as well.

As though inspired by the melody, Sparky pricked up his ears, and in a flash, he galloped toward the steps leading to the verandah, his frisky tail beating in rhythm to the allegro movement.

'Sparky,' I called hoarsely, 'Doc doesn't want to be disturbed! You'll get in trouble!'

But Sparky was on a lark and there was no stopping him. Up he climbed until he reached the screen door, and pushing it open with his head, he pranced right in, startling my father, who just then was sipping his usual Canadian Club whisky and water. Breathless, I ran behind the intruder hoping to catch him before some catastrophe took place, but I was not quick enough. He stood eye to eye with my father, and before I knew what was happening, he shamelessly stuck his muzzle right into Doc's glass, his big pink tongue slurping the golden liquid like it was a cocktail prepared just for him! I held my breath, but Doc just started laughing,

'Well, I'll be damned!' he exclaimed. 'The next time my wife complains about me having a drink, I'll have to tell her that what's good for the horse is good for the doctor!'

After that, Sparky followed his own ritual. Every evening without fail, he would visit Mr Bunyan where his sweet tooth was satisfied, and then climbing those steps to seventh heaven, he would rendezvous with my father, listening to Brahms, Beethoven and Mozart. Sometimes, I was sure I saw him swaying recklessly down to his stall, once the cocktails were over.

Reminiscing, I realize how serious I was as a girl, often

fearful of saying or doing the wrong thing. In me, there was a tension that resisted letting go. I was a worrier even then; a trait which deprived me of the childish joy so often found in the young. Sparky, on the other hand, was one to follow his bliss. He was unquenchable in his quest for pleasure and freedom, and yet he understood when the tempering of his wild side was called for.

He was a four-legged master, who raced into my heart and asked me to think outside the box, and untie the bonds of my own insecurity. Every animal, like every human being, is unique, and as we gallop through this earthly sojourn, respect, compassion and above all, humour, are the first-aid kit items needed for the fantastic ride.

Mother Merle

Merle was a mother to me for the longest time. I loved that woman. Just the sound of her name, Merle. I used to stretch it out on my tongue and roll it over my lips. It reminded me of Pearl. God knows Merle was a pearl. Not the delicate, white Japanese kind, but the solid, round black pearls that have a sheen and strength all of their own. I don't remember when I began calling her Mother Merle, but the name stuck. To this day, people still call her that. In her own private way, she nurtured me. Many were the times that I would slip into the steamy kitchen, heavy with the swirling aroma of fried chicken, peas 'n rice and Johnnie cake, and hunker down in the corner next to the broom cupboard. The little stepladder there was always open, and I could sit, resting my elbows on my knees, and watch her large frame move lightly through the kitchen. She was heavy and her belly protruded out from under the folds of her wide, cotton skirt, but boy, was she ever nimble. There was a youthful spring in her step. Her flat, oversized feet were haphazardly shoved into men's sandals, but she could do a merengue jig that made her look like a

teenager, and made me clap my hands in delight.

My informal education was undoubtedly augmented by the generous wisdom of this woman. I learned how to make sumptuous soul foods like boiled fish and grits. I saw how dangerously hot the Wesson oil needed to be, before the small yellowtail snappers could be fried.

'If dis oil ain't boilin' hot,' she would say above the sizzling pops, 'your fish goin' stick to de pan and den dey goin' fall apart and dey ain't goin' be cripsy. You understand, child?'

I would nod in agreement, quite certain, however, that when I grew up, Merle would be there to fry my fish and prevent the backs of my hands from becoming fields of blisters. The oil just never seemed to burn her.

Aside from her culinary knowledge, the subject of men was one that always enthralled her, and she enthusiastically sought to enlighten me in this regard.

'Gal,' she would say, 'when you find yourself to be a woman, don't you be marryin' no bad head man, you hear? Most o' dem men ain't no good! You gotta find one who goin' take care o' you. Not like my husband, who does go round drinkin' and carryin' on all night, and den come home wantin' sumptin' from me!'

Of course at my young age, I had no idea what 'sumptin' was and I would ask, 'What does he want Mother Merle? Isn't he tired when he comes home late?'

Throwing back her head, she would stand, legs spread wide, arms akimbo, and let loose a laugh that ranged from a deep rumble to a buoyant giggle and all the while her tummy would jiggle along merrily in tempo. Her laughter was so contagious that soon, I too would be holding my sides to stop them from splitting.

One evening, as I was just savouring one of her crispy chicken legs, she started to tell me a story.

'Gal,' she said in a tone that signified a great tale was about to unfold, 'sometimes, you gotta put de men dem in dey place!'

'What do you mean?' I asked curiously, wiping the grease from my lips in anticipation of what was to come.

'Well,' she said, busily salting the rest of the raw chicken, 'when I was a young woman, I worked as a cook in Nassau at de British Colonial Hotel. I was hard workin' and my mind wasn't on no foolishness.

'Even so, one of de waiters keep comin' into de kitchen and brushin' up against me, rubbin' up on my backside and whisperin' foolishness in my ear. I told him plain, to stop, but he ain't want listen. So one mornin', I was choppin' up de onion and de sweet green pepper for some steam fish, and he come behind me again, wrappin' his arms roun' my waist. I push his hand away, and I tell him if he do dat one more time I goin' get mad and he goin' get hurt!'

Pausing for a moment, as if to recall the situation, she dropped another chicken breast into the deep fryer, watching as it turned a golden brown.

'Go on, Mother Merle!' I urged.

'Well, dat boy was lookin' for trouble 'cause dat same week he come round again, only dis time he rub up on my waist and grab my bubbies and start to squeeze em! Child, ain't nobody goin' touch my bubbies unless I say so! Lucky for him, I ain't had no knife in my hand, cause sure as I talkin' to you now, I mighta kill him! Slice him up like salt pork!'

She stirred the rice and I thought I saw a fleeting look of remorse cross her face.

'What did you do to him, Mother Merle?'

'Gal, well he was laughin' up in my face, and he juck up my vexation so much, dat I turn and grab hold of his you know what!'

'His what?' I cried.

She pointed to the area between her legs, and my eyes grew as wide as saucers.

'He start yelpin' for me to let him go, but I was so vex dat I drag him right across de kitchen floor, pullin' dat ting with ev'ry ounce of strength in my body. I leave him in a heap right outside de door! De ambulance had to come and take him away!'

By now I was awed by my housekeeper's power, if not a little afraid.

'Did he die?' I asked fearfully.

'Almost,' she said a bit sorrowfully. 'To tell you de truth, I ain't proud of what I did, but he had me so mad! De next day, I gone see him in de hospital, and he tell me dat even under his blackberry skin he was all bruise up! De doctor tell him he lucky he ain't bleed to death inside hisself! I tell him I was sorry, and he say he was sorry too, he shouldn't have been foolin' with me like dat.'

'Did he ever try to touch you again?' I asked.

'Oh no, darlin! When he come back to work, he used to grin and make a big circle to avoid me.'

I remember mentally filing this story away under Things To Do If Accosted By A Man. I smile to think that, of the many experiences she talked about, this one remains indelibly printed in my memory. What a unique character she was, my Mother Merle! So jolly and spirited, and at the same time so imbued with a deep-rooted earnestness. On days when I ran to her, seething with rage because of some slapping injustice

hurled at me by one of my older brothers, she would hold me in her ample arms and say,

'Child, you gotta kiss ass, until you can kick it!'—an aphorism which allowed me repeatedly to face my tormentors with the inner resolution that, one day, I too would be victorious. It seems to me that these are the heartbeats of life, which make us who we are; unrecorded moments that form character.

My mentor, Merle, came complete with surprises. One of her eccentricities was the wearing of a wig. I never realized this until, one day, my father came into the kitchen to tell her he was going on a short trip to Miami. She stopped scrubbing the metal sink and said,

'Doc, if you is goin' off for a couple days, I wonder if you could bring me back a new wig?'

I gasped! 'A wig? Mother Merle, you wear a wig?'

Setting down the can of Ajax, she pulled off her hair, revealing a head of tight plaits. For me, it was an unforgettable moment, because this woman who carried herself with an air of confidence and majesty, suddenly looked bare and vulnerable. It never occurred to me that her black bob, which sported a straight fringe, was fake. Children never notice such things, or at least I didn't. Her hair lay crumpled in her hand, and I was disconcerted because it appeared to be such a forlorn and lifeless ball, nothing like the vibrant face that it adorned.

'Well, Merle, I hope I can find one that looks good and fits properly,' my father said, smiling broadly as he imagined himself in a store asking for wigs.

'My head ain't too big,' she said somewhat embarrassed. 'Maybe a medium size will do. I'm sure what you bring back goin' be jus' fine.'

And she popped her old wig right back on her head, pushing and fiddling with it until it was in place, and then she turned and went back to her cleaning. I, on the hand, sat on my stepladder in a state of unexpected disillusionment, aware for the first time that what you see isn't always what you get, but relieved that she was back in normal garb again.

I loved her as she was. I really did. For a chubby, freckle-faced girl filled with both promise and trepidation, she was a harbour of safety, embracing my dreams and my fears with candor. My own mother, who was strong and critical, could pierce me to the core. Running into Mother Merle's warm kitchen, I would always find assurance and fresh ways of looking at things.

'Your Ma only wantin' de best for you child! Yeah, dat's true, sometimes she run off her mouth 'cause she tired workin' so hard next to your Daddy, but God knows she love you plenty!'

Holding me close, soothing my childish spirit, she would melt me into her heart of grace like butter in an old iron skillet.

Sand In My Shoes

The Egret

Running through the village that day over the hot asphalt pavement, my bare feet were on fire. I turned the corner of the road leading up to our hill, and suddenly, I stopped dead in my tracks. The sound of vicious laughter filtered through the thick jungle bushes beside me. I paused, frightened by the cruelty in the words I heard behind the green curtain.

'Pull off his wings! Let's see if that dumb bird can fly when his wings are gone!'

The same voice hollered,

'What's the matter with you? You scared to pull' em off? Come on! Do it before he pecks a hole in your hand. Wait! Lemme smash his beak with this Coca-Cola bottle.'

An unseen force took hold of me, urging me forward through the knotted branches of dark speckled poison wood trees. Numb to the stones bruising my feet and the thorns scratching my arms, I pressed on, for once, unafraid of the huge spiders whose mighty webs wrapped themselves around my cheeks. Clawing the threads away from my eyes, I saw only red. Deep, dark, flaming red. Nothing could have stopped me.

It surprises me now when I look back. I was just nine years old, but I was consumed by a wrath so murderously righteous, that the culprits were completely taken by surprise.

As I burst into a clearing, I came upon two local boys. One of them was holding a BB gun and a Coca-Cola bottle, while the other boy was violently jerking the wings of a struggling bird, whose sleek, white feathers were now streaked with blood. More red. More rage.

The bird was fighting for his life, frantically pecking at his captor, his thin neck twisting grotesquely in the air.

'Give me that bird, you monsters!' I shrieked. Marching up to the churl holding the bird, I snatched it from his hands.

I was not only cross, I was furious at the violence displayed by these kids! This anger was my saving grace, for they both became momentarily ashamed.

'Hey, we was just teasin' the bird!' one boy said.

'Teasing?' I stormed. 'If someone broke your arms, would you call that teasing? You guys are sick!'

Not giving them time to change their minds, I disappeared back through the bushes, holding the fluttering animal in my hands.

'You better not come after this bird,' I hollered, 'or the next time you need to see my Daddy, I'll tell him to give you a needle as big as a shark hook and so crooked that it'll tear the flesh right off your backsides!'

Suddenly, I was alone with a bird that was not about to recognize me as his good Samaritan. His heart was pounding against my palms, and his yellow beak pierced the skin on my fingers, drawing blood, but determination propelled me forward. I knew this bird needed help. He had been shot through the wing, and would surely have been killed by a cat or a dog if I let him go, so I continued to run home, up the hill, refusing to succumb to his angry pecking.

I'm not really all that brave. I wonder if I would be able to conquer my fear and perform such a random act of courage now that I'm older. In all honesty, I'm even frightened of handling our tiny parakeet, lest he tweak the back of my hand. I'm a coward when it comes to holding birds; a trait which was magnified by my mother's total fearlessness of the species.

My mother was a bird woman. She could identify any bird that flew in the sky, each song that twittered through the air, and all the eggs in the trees and on the ground.

Sometimes, when we walked along the rocky shoreline, she would tug at my sleeve and whisper,

'Look! Can you see that swallow nesting in the ground?'

I was so myopic that just seeing the outline of the camouflaged bird was a miracle.

'Watch her now! She will fly to another spot to divert our attention away from her eggs.'

Those were wonderful times, walking with my mother, holding her hand, hearing the warm excitement in her voice when she spotted a bird. At other times, she would race into my room at sunrise and haul me out of bed.

'Come quickly!' she would whisper. 'There are two parrots sitting in the poinciana tree outside my bedroom! You need to see what they look like and hear their voices! This bird is called *amazonis leucocephala bahamensis*! And do you know what's so wonderful about it?'

'No,' I would moan, rubbing the sleep out my eyes.

'It's the only parrot that nests in subterranean rock cavities!'

'What does that mean?' I'd ask sleepily.

'That means they nest in the ground. There are only two islands in The Bahamas where this New World parrot breeds: Abaco and Inagua. But in Inagua they nest in trees.'

'Why?' I asked, suddenly curious.

'I think it's because the trees in Abaco have fewer holes, and so the bird has adapted to the ground. Isn't that amazing?'

I saw in her a passion that was remarkable. To her dying day, she fought valiantly to save the Bahamian parrot—painting posters, raising funds, and launching a single-handed campaign to wipe out the stray wildcats that were a menace to the parrot chicks sitting helplessly in shallow burrows in the ground. She sweet-talked the hunters, explaining that parrots were not a delicacy, but a national treasure; she begged them not to catch the birds and sell them for a few dollars, often buying a captured parrot with her own money and releasing it back into the wild. When she saw that the hunters continued their ignorant ways, her kind lectures turned into torrents of wrath! She was a fearless pioneer, a woman of justice, but because she was also the nurse, the one who administered injections and helped my father mete out the medicine, no one wanted to be cursed by her.

Now, as I raced up the stairs clutching the wounded bird, I prayed that she would be there.

'Mummy! Mummy! Come quick!' I cried as I dashed onto the verandah.

'What is it?' she asked, hurrying out of the kitchen.

'I have a bird. Some boys were trying to kill it! He's bleeding. I'm scared he might die!' After a moment, I added. 'I'm scared because he's pecking my hand.'

I don't know who was trembling more, the bird or me.

Gently, she lifted the bird from my hands, crooning soft

words of reassurance.

'What have they done to you, my feathered friend?' she asked as she set about examining his wounds.

In her skillful hands, the bird quieted down. I watched in awe as her nimble fingers gently probed his battered body.

'Oh, my poor baby, they have broken your wing. You will need time to heal. I hope you will fly again.'

Cradling the bird in her arms, she set about creating a safe resting place. A large cardboard box was retrieved from the greenhouse and lined with a soft towel. A dish of water containing antibiotic drops was placed nearby, and when everything was prepared, she lowered the bird into his hospital bed. He was still, his beady eyes warily checking out the new surroundings.

'Do you know what type of bird this is?' my mother asked.

'I think it's a Great Egret.' I replied shyly, nervous lest I was wrong.

She looked at me, and suddenly, my young heart swelled to see the gleam of admiration in her eyes. There is something about that gleam in a mother's eye that touches every child on a non-verbal level. I believe it is what nurtures a child's psyche. It is just as important as mother's milk, and when it is lacking, one part of the child's soul goes hungry. There are no words that can take the place of one shining glance filled with a parent's recognition. She was proud of me and I knew it.

She asked me to tell her how I had saved the bird. As I recounted the story, her admiration grew, and I basked in the sunlight streaming from her face. Praise is a gift to children. No, it is a prerequisite for healthy development, and too often, parents forget the wonderful effect it can have on the

young. But this day, I got my fill and I fell in love with that bird. Now, I really wanted him to survive.

He made it through the first night. However, in the morning a problem arose. He would not eat. I tried everything from freshly minced hamburger meat to tasty fish filets, but nothing whet his appetite. He swiveled his head from side to side, regarding me with a blank stare as if to say,

'You don't expect me to eat that, do you?'

I was becoming anxious. He needed nourishment. Even my mother, who knew everything about birds, was disturbed, and wondered why he would not eat any of the delicacies we served him.

'Perhaps he doesn't want us to watch him eating,' she suggested, but when we returned a few hours later, the fish and hamburger were feeding only a frenzied line of ants.

'Mummy, what are we going to do?' I wailed.

She shook her head thoughtfully.

Another night passed. At sunrise, I rushed out to check on my egret. He sat quietly in his box, but I could see that he was becoming weaker. He was apathetic and no longer fidgeted when I approached, a sign that his strength was ebbing.

'What do you want to eat?' I whispered. 'I promise to get you whatever you want, but you need to give me a clue.'

Just then, a lizard scurried out of a potted plant. The egret's head shot up with lightening speed, his eyes suddenly alert and bright. He flapped his injured wings in a futile attempt to get out of the box, while the lizard took one look at him and flew into hiding.

'No!' I exclaimed in horror. 'You eat live lizards!'

By this time, I wasn't so sure that I wanted to become the accomplice of a lizard killer, but I wanted the bird to survive.

Besides, there were thousands of lizards in our garden and only one egret, so I knew what Nature demanded of me. After all, I had made a promise. Nevertheless, I was in a dilemma. I loved lizards and I loved the egret. There was no way that I was going to catch lizards in a glass and feed them to my friend. Not that I was unable to do this task, I was certainly capable. As children, we caught hundreds of lizards in jars, but I had always released them after studying them for some time. I did not have the guts to make this a gladiator sport with me playing Caesar! Looking at the bird I said,

'You know what? We'll make this a fair game. I'll take you into the garden, but you must catch your own lizards. Okay?'

The egret blinked. Slowly, I lifted him from the box and carried him outside where the purple bougainvillea bushes bloomed high, and the crab grass was thick and crunchy. Setting him down, I watched him shake his feathers. I was afraid that he might be weak from the loss of blood, but within seconds, his graceful neck was elongated and his entire body took on the energy of a stealthy hunter. Thin legs silently stalked the invisible prey. The deliberate elegance with which he moved was mesmerizing. All focus now, nothing else existed except his intention to feed. Head swaying to and fro, he mimicked the undulating rhythm of his prey in an ancient survival ritual. Swiftly, his sleek head plunged forward, the sharp beak stabbing the unsuspecting reptile warming itself in the sun. The kill was precise and calculated. I had to admire him for that. No indecision, just pure hunter's instinct. Fascinated, I watched as the lizard was lifted upwards and quickly thrown back into the hungry gullet.

Honestly, it disturbed me to see the lizard still wriggling as

he travelled down his predator's throat into a dark cavern of death, but what to do? Nature feeds upon Nature. We kill to live, and now, in some strange way, by saving a life I had become an accomplice to death. In that very moment, I was struck by the duality of existence. We cannot have life without death. There is no light without darkness. We cannot be satiated unless we have known hunger. Something is always sacrificed to maintain balance. It was a profound lesson for a young girl; one that I have never forgotten and one that has helped me cope when I felt unjustly treated by the hand of fate.

And so it was that I took my egret for walks every day, leading him to those secret spots where hordes of lizards lived. I knew every hidden lizard hotel because the garden was my playground. Sometimes we strolled down to the coconut grove where the fat curly tails lived. I would sit on the bent trunk of a coconut tree, jutting out over the water while he hunted. He never went after the big lizards though. Perhaps the smaller ones were tastier. What a peculiar sight we made; the chubby girl and her slender companion.

One day my mother said,

'Sweetheart, I need to talk to you. Your egret's wing is nearly mended now. Soon he will want to fly away and find his friends.'

'No!' I cried. 'He won't fly away and leave me! I'm his friend now!'

However, soon after, I noticed my egret stretching his wings as if to test their span. He did not fly, but I saw in him a new restlessness. His shiny eyes scanned the blue sky, and my heart sank because I felt his longing to ride the wind. I knew I could never travel with him, and this saddened me. He had become so much a part of my daily routine. He was

the reason I raced home after school. He was the one I talked to when we wandered among the grapefruit trees. He was the one who taught me to step lightly through the grass and wait in silence. Through him, I became rooted in the dimension of inner stillness, learning to perceive the underlying consciousness in every flower, tree or form. His presence attuned me to the sustaining force in all things. There is a magic that happens when children and creatures communicate. No words are needed.

One evening at sunset, when the sky was on fire, I sat on the garden wall watching him at his favourite pastime. The pond, adorned with fragrant water lilies, had become another hunting ground. In addition to lizards, he now relished the taste of fresh guppies. It intrigued me to see him wade through the water, flicking his yellow feet to startle his prey. As soon as a fish or frog tried to avoid this intrusion, the egret's beak would become an effective spear.

Suddenly, I heard the beating of wings. I looked up to see another snowy white egret land beneath the old ficus tree. Instantly, my bird became alert, his body quivering in anticipation. Hopping out of the pond, he sauntered toward the newcomer and began to circle her at a distance. His neck stretched upwards and outwards, demanding her attention, while his bill called to her with soft, snapping noises. I experienced a rush of mixed emotions, so touched was I by the astonishing beauty of both birds standing in the dusk and the heart-wrenching fact that they belonged together. I knew my time with my egret was over. He was never my egret. He was only a winged traveller on my path, one who entrusted me with the gift of friendship for a brief while. I watched him now, communing with his own kind, the injured wing trembling with a new sense of adventure. My heart felt lonely, yet full.

A soft hand touched my shoulder. My mother stood beside me, her voice a lullaby on the evening breeze.

'We can never hold those we love back from life. The more we love, the more we must let go.'

Wiping my eyes I whispered,

'I understand, but it hurts.'

She nodded knowingly.

Just then, the two birds took flight. At first, I wondered whether my friend would make it. Flapping his wings precariously, he fought for balance, his body slipping sideways. Then suddenly, as though supported by a mysterious wind, he rose and soared through the indigo sky, white gossamer feathers creating a shower of light that moved with faith into the unknown darkness.

Sand In My Shoes

Eating Curbs

When I was a young girl, collecting curbs was a favourite pastime. I'm not talking about the curbs that frame our streets —I'd have a hard time gathering those in my pockets. I'm referring to a different kind, the mollusk kind. Now, I have searched both the Oxford and the American dictionaries for the word 'curb,' seeking a definition that might relate to any kind of sea creature, but this quest has been unsuccessful. However, you ask any Bahamian and they will tell you that curbs were once a national delicacy.

Sadly, these little creatures, also known as chitons, hardly grace our shores any longer. One needs to visit the small, uninhabited cays to find such an animal, and even then, they are a rare occurrence. This makes me wonder how fast our world is changing.

I mean, I'm not a limping old beachcomber yet. It hasn't been that long since I climbed over the sharp rocks on Abaconian shores, struggling to keep my balance on the slippery algae. What happened to those tiny mollusks that were so abundant in every crevice washed clean by the surging tides?

Why do they no longer hide beneath the rocks in pools of shallow water? They were so easy to find, and ever so hard to pry loose. One small curb, only a few millimeters long, could adhere to a rock with the strength of Samson. Concealed beneath eight arched mini plates, they would clamp their bellies onto the face of a rock with unequalled vigour. No one had fingers strong enough to dislodge one of those mighty miniatures.

It saddens me to remember what we, as children, did when we went on the hunt for these precious invertebrates. Sharp knives were the tools of destruction. Why did I follow the others, and do something I abhorred? I wasn't mindful then. And I was afraid of being excluded. Succumbing to peer pressure, I would slip the glinting blade in between the creature's underbelly and the mossy rock, and pry it away from the surface it clung to with such tenure. Then swiftly, I would cut away at the soft fleshy part of the mollusk, separating it from the round segmented shell, which was its protective home. I really wasn't mindful then! I did not walk with respect for these small organisms that have inhabited our planet for some five hundred million years. Afraid of being ostracized by the group, I became the ruthless killer of another group. I did not heed the small voice within. The voice that urges each one of us to respect nature's tiniest sparks.

Usually, there was a bunch of us combing the rocky shoreline, and most of the kids were older than I. They drank Bacardi Rum mixed with coke and lime. Because I was the youngest, I had the job of slicing the limes for their drinks and for the curb marinade. The sting would sear through my arms when the acid touched the scrapes on my fingers. I had so many cuts from holding on to the rocky needles that were my only

support when I felt myself from slipping. I would rush to the sea and rinse my hands in the salt water; but the pain stayed with me. Squeezing that lime juice over the naked curbs, I waited, watching them curl up like ribbons, their flesh poaching in the pungent liquid. I still feel the burn in my heart.

As a child, the thought of eating living flesh was frightening. But even more frightening was the thought of being shunned by the group. Eating raw curbs was a ritual that demanded courage, and a whole new set of table manners. Chewing the rubbery substance spiced with salt and hot goat pepper, I wondered all the while if the curbs in my mouth could actually feel the fire, and my teeth. Were they hurting too? What a strange thing to ponder. I felt concern for those tiny creatures suffering between my molars, but everyone else was eating them and raving. Fresh was best! The spicier, the better. Raw curbs were the pinnacle of Bahamian cuisine!

I knew that if the others glimpsed one moment of squeamishness, they would laugh at me, and call me a coward. So, chewing bravely, I faked enjoyment, pretending that nothing could make me cringe—not even curbs wiggling like caterpillars around my tongue. I was a big girl. I could handle anything. No one was going to tell me I couldn't run with the in-crowd.

I am older now. Not quite as nimble on the rocks. I don't care about the in-crowd. And, I am more mindful. Life has taught me that reverence for all things is a gift, primarily to myself. Now, when I follow the line of rocks along the tide, I dream of seeing one more chiton gleaming in the wet sun. I realize that, of all the creatures in this world, we are the lost ones. We have torn our hearts away from the earth, away from the ocean. In our mad desire for more, we have heated

our globe with dead passion, stealing everything we can from paradise, and dumping our leftovers, with little consideration for our friends.

Today, if I were blessed enough to see one tiny curb, I would bend my ear to the slimy rocks and try to hear what this miniature warrior has to say; this ancient mariner who has crept along the time line of the centuries, gathering secrets at a snail's pace. Perhaps, I too would learn to move with greater deliberation, and chew my food more slowly, savouring each mouthful with reverence, as though it were my last.

Tales of

Unlikely Heroes

Guava and Alphonse

Alphonse Rolle was a shy boy. His shyness was magnified by the fact that he had an insatiable curiosity and love for pigs. This trait led to merciless teasing by the other children in the village of Dundas Town in Abaco, an island nestled in the turquoise waters of the northern Bahamas. Alphonse was fascinated by the rotund animals, with their pink faces, squinting eyes and curly, wiggling tails.

Although he seldom spoke around people, Alphonse would chatter away like a wild parrot when he was near pigs. He was sure that they understood every word he uttered, because when he looked into their eyes, he saw such wisdom and humour that he could not contain himself from sharing his deepest joys and sorrows.

Some days, he would race home after school, his bare, calloused feet flying over the rocky path, winding its way down the hill from the wind-battered schoolhouse to the rickety homemade pigpen in his yard. Often, the other children would toss mango skins at him, and laughing loudly, they would shout,

'Hey, Alphonse Rolle, these are for your pigs, but make sure you don't eat them, or you might turn into a roley poley yourself! Oink! Oink!'

Alphonse would catch the slimy peels, and holding them in his hands like a treasure, he would leap over the fence, calling out the name of his most cherished pig.

'Come here, Guava! You get first pick!'

Guava would dance circles around him, nuzzling his legs with her warm snout until he bent down and gave her the treat. The other pigs seemed quite aware of the hierarchy in the pen, and freely granted Guava the rights to her queenly position.

Alphonse loved the feeling of mud squashing up between his toes, the sour smell of pig muck, but more than this, he loved listening to the knowing grunts emanating from the pigs' bellies when he whispered his dreams and tribulations into their ears. It was inconceivable to him that the pigs were not responding to his words. On some level, he simply knew that a language existed between him and the animals, and he implicitly trusted their insights concerning his life. Sometimes, they would squeal with laughter or moan sadly. At other times their grunts would come out in fast, high-pitched staccatos, warning him to take action. If they wanted to soothe his vexed spirit, they would croon to him in slow, vibrating arpeggios. Guava was especially proficient in conversing with Alphonse, and that was why he loved her most.

Guava was celebrating her second birthday when Alphonse came home one day. He recalled the day exactly, because it was the day school closed for the summer. Excited, he rushed into his mother's tiny kitchen asking,

'Ma, did you bake the cake?'

His mother stood with her hands on her broad hips, her apron sprinkled with flour.

'Child, I baked you a cake, but I am worried that you are growing too attached to that pig. Daddy says it's time to bring Guava to the chopping block.'

Alphonse felt weak. His knobby knees began to tremble, and all the blood drained from his small, dark face to fill a pounding heart. His throat closed, and his mother could see the nervous flutter in the hollow of his neck. Overcome with tenderness for her boy, she moved to embrace him, pulling his woolly head to her bosom. Deep in her heart, she recognized his spirit, his love for creatures and natural things, which set him apart from all the tough boys in the village, running about, kicking the mongrel dogs or senselessly killing small banana quits with their slingshots. Alphonse abhorred any act of cruelty, and Margarita Rolle worried that life's harsh lessons would leave him broken. He was her only child. Unlike all the other native women bearing six or more children, Margarita had conceived only one boy, and this, after twelve years of trying and praying. She had wept when he came into the world; a scrawny, sickly, stick-like baby. She was very protective of him, indulging his whims behind her husband's back. It worried her that her husband thought the boy was weak and unmanly.

'That boy needs to toughen up. He will never be a man if he keeps sweet-talkin' pigs all day long!' he would complain.

'He'll be all right,' she would answer placidly. 'Just give him some time.'

Yet, with those words, her nerves felt as fragile as the sand dollars that broke beneath her feet when she walked the beach.

'Ma,' he whispered, 'please don't let him take Guava. He

can have my plate of food for the rest of my life. Please, Ma,' he begged.

'Darling, I'm going to do what I can. Hush now! Take this cake and have your little party with Guava.'

Alphonse ran off, holding the cake, two little birthday candles soon melting onto the icing, like teardrops.

Summer passed in a hot haze. Every day, Alphonse would go to the old hand pump, balancing his bucket on the rocks, pumping it full of water until the pail overflowed. Then he would carry the heavy load back to the pigsty and delight in splashing the cool liquid all over the animals' backs. He found an old bristle brush and scrubbed Guava until her pink flesh gleamed. In the afternoons, he would escort her out of the pen and go for long walks on the beach. When the heat became unbearable, they would both bask in the cool sea, where Alphonse never tired of throwing his arms about the pig's neck and having her tow him back to shore. Later, they would find hidden paths where coco plums grew in wild abundance, and Guava would rotate her mobile snout, sniffing out the best plums and eating her fill.

They were completely content, the boy and the pig, but the village elders often remarked to Margarita,

'It ain't right. Your boy ain't got no friends except for dat pig.' Margarita would nod and continue on, praying silently for something to change.

Alphonse's father was a skilled captain, a man well known for handling schooners, and sailing through any kind of storm. His crew nicknamed him 'Capt Directly' because he gave strict and direct orders, and never failed to bring the sleek ship directly into harbour, no matter how gray or torrential the sky. However, Capt Directly carried a secret

fear that he would never have dreamed of telling a soul. He feared that one day he would lose his sixth sense and flounder out on the open seas, far away from land. He was afraid that his intuitive gift for finding land would someday diminish, and he would die in shame, searching for dry ground. The idea that a blanket of clouds could thwart his ability to follow the stars or the sun, gnawed at his self worth, making him cranky and often impatient. This doubt grew like a terrible mound filled with stinging ants, burning away in his gut, under his cocky exterior.

One evening, at the end of the summer, a few weeks before school was to reopen, the Rolle family sat at the table, sipping coconut water from glass jars. Alphonse's father was headed out the following day, on a trip to New Providence, to pick up supplies for the owner of the schooner, who was a merchant. The trip would take about ten days.

'Pa,' Alphonse asked nervously, 'could I come with you tomorrow? I'd be back in time for school.'

Capt Directly started to bark a sharp no, but something in the boy's eyes made him swallow the word. He saw a yearning and a need for acceptance, and this made his heart soften.

'All right, son,' he said gruffly, 'I'm going down to the docks at four o'clock in the morning. You come on board at five thirty, just before sunrise, and then we'll high-tail it out of the harbour on the tide. Don't be late now, or I'll have to leave without you.'

It was still dark the next morning when Alphonse kissed his mother goodbye. She watched him leave through the front door, dragging his large, green duffel bag behind him.

'You got enough clothes, boy?' she asked, noticing how little was in the bag.

'Yeah, Ma. I won't be needing much.' And before she could ask the next question that every mother asks, he added,

'Don't worry, I have my toothbrush!'

With that, he disappeared into the street. What she did not know was, that a few minutes later, he crept along the side of the little wooden cottage, back to the pigpen, and under his breath, he ordered the pigs not to make a sound. Then he opened the rusty latch, which he had oiled the night before with Crisco lard, and nudged Guava out. Together, they disappeared into the gray dawn, careful not to take the street through the village, but running along the overgrown paths, down to the docks where the old schooner lay waiting.

Just before reaching their destination, Alphonse sat down on a rock and told Guava his plan.

'You are going to have to be very quiet,' he said in a commanding whisper. 'No talking, until you are safely stowed away on the boat.'

Guava turned her head back and forth as though she were listening intently. Her eyes searched the boy's face in the dim light, attempting to discern every facial expression.

'I know you're not crazy about being picked up, but I have to stick you in this bag, and you must be still.'

A short time later, members of the crew saw the captain's boy come on board carrying a stoutly filled duffel bag. Alphonse was directed below deck, where he stayed until the boat left the harbour. He was tired from the previous night's excitement, and fell asleep on the bunk, with Guava cuddled in his lap.

Several hours later, he was awakened by loud roaring and squealing. His father stood in the small cabin holding Guava by the ample folds of skin on her neck, shouting angrily,

'Damn! You are one crazy boy! You brought this pig along

without telling me?'

Alphonse nodded mutely.

'I feel so ashamed!' his father shouted. 'What the hell am I going to do with a pig cavorting all round my ship?' And with his free hand, he began cuffing Alphonse behind the ears.

Guava's squeals became hysterical when she saw her friend being beaten. Wriggling furiously, she managed to twist out of her captor's hand and land feet first on the floor, where she turned to charge him with such vehemence, that he toppled over onto his son.

Struggling in a most ungainly fashion, the captain managed to stand up, and cursing like a madman, heaved himself through the narrow cabin door, slamming it behind him. Shaken, Alphonse looked at his pig and said,

'This is serious, Guava. My daddy is one angry man. We better lay low for a while!'

Nodding her head in agreement, Guava oinked nervously.

The schooner was making great headway riding on the stiff breeze that had blown up out of the east. Alphonse and his companion spent the day and the next night in the cabin, hoping to avoid the captain's wrath, but in the morning of the second day, the inseparable two gathered their courage and decided to go on deck. They were both feeling queasy from the stuffy cabin air and the pitching motion of the ship. Alphonse had fashioned a leash out of a frayed piece of rope, which he tied around the pig's neck, hoping to keep her secure.

On deck, all hands were busy, and the tension was palpable. The sails billowed out, ropes and winches were being tightened, and the wind tore at the boy's face. Above him, the clouds had formed an ominous black mountain. Rain began to pelt down in heavy sheets, and Alphonse was hardly

able to see his pig just inches away from his leg. Claps of thunder shattered the air. With each earsplitting blast, Guava would freeze, holding her breath in sheer terror. She felt panicked by the loud noise, and kept turning her head to figure out where the din was coming from. She wanted to run but the rope restrained her.

Clutching the rail with one hand, Alphonse inched toward the helm where he knew his father would be commanding the ship. Every now and then, he would drop to his knees and inch forward on all fours, fearful of being swept overboard. His father stood hunched against the weather, his calloused hands gripping the wheel, which seemed to have a mind of its own, as it spun wildly in every direction.

The first mate stood next to the captain, and Alphonse heard him shout,

'Capt Directly, dis one killer storm comin' up. I could feel dat in my bones! De wind got dat special smell!'

Alphonse looked up at his father, and saw something he had never seen before. For one fleeting moment, Capt Directly's face was haunted with a fear so pure and unmistakable, that it harrowed up the boy's soul, leaving him utterly distressed. Until now, Alphonse had never doubted his father's capabilities, but suddenly, he was filled with dread. He could not know that his father's worst nightmare was becoming a reality.

Turning on the child with unleashed fury, the captain hissed,

'Get out of my sight, boy! It's you who have brought me this bad luck. You and that goddamn pig!'

Kicking Guava, he sent her sprawling along the slippery deck. Both the pig and the boy crawled away on all fours toward the bow, where they found a protected niche and held on for dear life.

The crew also felt that something had gone askew. Their

captain, normally so sure of himself, seemed different, agitated. His orders were incoherent, and the seamen felt that he no longer knew where he was going, and of course, this was the terrible truth. Capt Directly was rendered helpless by fear. Anxiety whirled in his chest, constricting his sense of self. He felt confused, and suddenly saw himself, a windblown moron, grasping the helm as a last shred of dignity. He could not even mouth a prayer because he felt that his soul was already lost beneath the raging surface of the sea, floundering in a watery hell.

The men were well trained and managed to steady the ship, doing what was necessary, but after hours of relentless pounding, not one of them knew where east or west lay. The wind began to lessen, bringing about an even greater feeling of hesitation and bewilderment; for while they were busy, the men felt useful, but now they were frightened because they did not know where they were. Some of them feared they might smash onto a great coral reef, and drown or be eaten by sharks. Others thought the currents might carry them to savage islands where cannibals would eat them alive. Each man harboured his own personal fear of death.

All through the night, the schooner was pulled along through the ocean. Not one star was visible in the soggy sky. Dawn arrived but the sun remained hidden. Still the men were helpless, but now they were becoming angry with their useless captain, who refused to utter one word, and stood bent over the wheel, a dazed and faraway look in his eyes.

'He mussee lose his mind,' one of the sailors said. 'Time for us to take over de ship, but I ain't sure where to go.'

Sailors are a superstitious lot, and this bunch was no exception. Suddenly, an unkempt deckhand stepped forward, a knife in his hand.

'I is telling yinna, de pig is de problem! Dat pig is carryin' obeah, and it done cast a spell on all o' us. My feelin' is, de time is here to kill it!' Then he added, 'I goin' ask de cook to make some pig's feet souse 'cause after all dis tossin' an' turnin', I is hungry!'

Alphonse was crouched low in the bow of the schooner, listening to all this. He knew that sailors were brutish, and would not hesitate to cut Guava's throat. Guava began to tremble, the mass of her pink body quivering, as she sensed the murderous energy. The men approached, cursing in vulgar tones. Alphonse knew that he had to make a swift decision. With the speed of lightning, he bolted forward, pulling his precious friend along, and then with one rapid movement, he grabbed her and heaved her over the high bow.

'Swim Guava! Swim home!' he cried, leaning his frail body over the ship's side. But seeing her alone in the purple water, his heart collapsed in grief, and he made yet another choice: to jump in after her. Everyone rushed to see what was going to happen. To the amazement of all, the pig waited unperturbed for her comrade, and when he was safely clinging to her neck, she brandished her snout in the air, and twitching it back and forth in a methodical fashion, she sniffed and sniffed until her nose seemed to point her in a definite direction. Without looking back at her attackers, she set off swimming on a course directly opposite to the one that the ship was taking.

On board, pandemonium broke out. The captain, seeing his son float away in the distance, was catapulted out of his stupor. Barking orders, he tacked sharply, bringing the hull around to follow the two heads that were disappearing in the distance.

Capt Directly felt as though a crushing weight had been lifted from his brow, and clarity returned. He knew, as sure as he was

still standing, that Guava was leading them ashore. The pig was so self-assured, so impervious to the depth of the ocean below. She was like a fat mermaid, driven by an invisible guiding force. Snout held high, she pushed forward, forcefully kicking her opulent haunches, yet ever so careful to maintain contact with the thin arms around her neck. She grunted reassuringly, in soft semi-tones, whenever Alphonse began to whimper. There was no stopping her. She was fed up with the uncomfortable ship and wanted dry land beneath her feet. When the sailors saw their own leader had come to his senses, they began to cheer, so relieved were they that order had been restored.

A hemp fishing net was cast overboard to haul Guava and Alphonse back on deck. The men crowded round the boy and the pig, chattering and singing their praises.

Sure enough, several hours later, following the navigational course that Guava had set, the old sailor, Sightman Archer, spied land, despite the growing glaucoma in his eyes. Grateful, they sailed into the quaint harbour of Nassau, the crew already dreaming of rum and plump women.

When they returned to Abaco, the tale of heroism spread like a bush fire. Alphonse was carried down the plank on his father's broad shoulders, wearing a smile as wide as the Caribbean Sea. Guava pranced proudly before them, a lei of red and yellow hibiscus adorning her corpulent neck.

The village children shoved their way to the front of the crowd, shouting,

'Welcome back, Alphonse! Can we come and play with your pig tomorrow?'

However, this time, they were not teasing; they truly wanted to touch a celebrity and a piece of valiant glory.

It is said that, for decades after, until the compass became

standard equipment on board, each ship that left Abaco and other harbours throughout the West Indies was outfitted with a pig that resided on the bow like a voluptuous figurehead. Well fed and tenderly cared for, these animals commanded respect.

Alphonse became a famous breeder of an aristocratic pig lineage. Blessed as they were with a keen sense of smell and bold wisdom, Guava's descendants continued to fetch the highest market price, and were renowned all over the world.

Peter and the Shark

Dusk was falling over the peaceful sea; streaks of orange bleeding into the purple sky. Peter gazed at the fading horizon, his green eyes roaming the water's surface, alert to any ripple that might break the stillness. His old, twenty-eight-foot long See Vee was securely anchored, the rods cast, eagerly awaiting the strike of a shark.

Fishing was Peter's expertise—no, it was more than that—it was his life, his passion. He lived on the water, and figured he would die there too. There was nothing about the sea that this crinkly necked man did not know. His hands and arms bore the mark of the ocean, hundreds of white, thread-like scars covered his skin, mirroring the sharp, spiny corals he had brushed up against while spearfishing in the waters below. Teeth marks and punctures, now tautly healed, conjured up vivid images of fish on tangled nylon lines, trashing about in the throes of death, fighting for one last breath, angry with their captor.

Peter was a quiet man. In fact, most people found him standoffish, even strange. The few friends he had, attempted to chastise him for fishing alone.

'Peter,' they would say, 'you know you should always have a buddy with you when you fish. Why do you put yourself at risk? Anything can happen out there.'

'I've been fishing alone all my life,' he would answer in his Bahamian drawl, tinged with a lilting accent that was part of his Scottish heritage. 'I don't know any different, and I'm not about to change now.'

There was a finality to his words, and no one dared to question him further.

Peter sat at the helm waiting patiently. He never drank alcohol while fishing, only small, pint sized bottles of purified water, which he kept chilled in the huge, ice filled coolers used to store the fish he caught. The silence of the evening filled him with a sense of peace. He felt at home on the sea; no one was able to irritate his solitude out here. Daily responsibilities of feeding his family seemed to lessen with the lapping of the waves. Tonight however, he felt hard-pressed to catch a shark. Lately, things had been tough; too many storms had stopped him from fishing. The bills were stacked high on the kitchen counter. Shark fishing was how he made his money, especially this time of year, but restaurant owners were complaining bitterly because he had not brought them a haul in weeks. Now they were threatening to take blackened shark off the menu for good if he could not supply their needs. He felt tired.

Suddenly, he heard the imperceptible sound of a fin slicing through water. He stood up, his lean body tense with antici-pation. The Penn rod on the starboard side of the boat whirred with a familiar, high-pitched sound. When fishing for sharks this way, Peter never removed the rod from the

holder on the side of the boat. His job was simply to reel in the fish, gaff it and haul it into the boat. The line buzzed as the fish began running.

'Run baby!' Peter said under his breath. 'Tire yourself out!'

Seconds later, he heard the fish jump out of the water. In the dim light, he could make out the form of a spinner shark, leaping and turning just above the surface before crashing down again into the liquid night. He knew how to play the shark, reeling it in when it was not running, and waiting while the fish tore off in the other direction. He had pulled in hundreds of this kind, feeling into the animal, becoming one with the muscle and power, sensing its next move. The excitement of the hunt never ceased to thrill him; the knowledge that, when fighting the beast, he had to remain calm and superior at all times.

Spinning into the air and splashing back into the water, the shark drew closer to the boat. Peter could see the fin racing wildly from side to side. He knew that he must bring the shark in close enough to club it. Spinner sharks were different, in that they needed to be weakened before being hauled into the boat, otherwise they could spin right into your face. Reeling in the line, he could make out the gray form of the shark now, right next to the boat. Peter reckoned he was five feet long, and about one hundred pounds.

A feisty teenager, he thought wryly.

Reaching out with his left hand, he pulled the leader wire closer to his body, while his right arm raised the blunt, wooden club, ready to smash down on the shark's head. Just at that moment, the shark ripped out of the water, his jaws headed straight for Peter's face. Surprised, the man stepped back, as he stared into the cold, expressionless eyes of his opponent.

In the chaos, Peter did not notice the leader wire wrapping itself around the index finger of his left hand, but as the shark fell back into the sea, Peter knew instantly that disaster had struck. His body lurched forward, somersaulting headfirst over the side of the boat into the inky water below. Struggling frantically, he brought himself into an upright position, forcing his head to the surface for one last breath of air, before being dragged down again. Immediately, he could feel the power of the enraged animal as its tail struck his face, pushing him further away from the safety of his boat.

Perhaps it was Peter's knowledge of the sea, or the fact that he had often imagined a scenario like this in his mind, that kept him from panicking; whatever it was, a cold, calculated desire for survival kicked into every cell of his being. He knew that the water was relatively shallow, seven feet deep at most, and as he went under, he was relieved to feel the sandy bottom under the rubber soles of his topsiders. Every muscle and sinew in his body strained to catapult him upwards, in the direction of the boat. The crazed shark was also fighting for freedom, shaking its powerful head back and forth, trying to rid itself of the cruel hook embedded in its mouth. There was no way that Peter could free his hand. The wire had cut through his flesh and tendons, and was now tightly looped around the bone of his index finger, keeping the shark firmly attached to his arm. Peter could not see anything, but he could taste the blood that flowed freely in the water from his severed artery. He knew that it was just a matter of time before other sharks smelled it too.

As his head broke the water's surface, he could see the running lights of his boat about forty feet away.

Fighting for his life, Peter tugged at the fish with every

ounce of human strength he possessed. He did not know how long he fought, but at some point, he began to gain ground, even though the angry shark bounced into him, bruising him and forcing him back under the surface. For Peter, it became a gladiator's dance. As the shark moved in to hit him, Peter allowed himself to be thrust underwater, each time his feet searching desperately for solid ground, so that he could push himself up, toward the safety of the boat.

Why the shark did not bite him was beyond his understanding. When he finally felt the fiberglass surface of his faithful Sea Vee and was able to hoist himself onto the smooth, diving platform near the stern, he gave thanks for the day that he decided to buy a boat with this particular amenity. Another boat, without a platform or ladder, would have meant certain death. Quickly, he jerked his legs upward, knowing that the shark would bite any dangling object.

What came next required total clarity and nerves of steel. Peter's finger, now almost completely severed, was held together by a thin piece of bone, and this, too, was crushed. He still needed to drag the shark in over the stern. Heaving his body backward, he hauled the trashing fish into the middle of the boat, groping for the club with his right hand. Luckily, his fingers found the handle, and raising his arm, he brought the weapon down again and again, crushing the menacing jaws, beating the shark into submission. Using wire cutters, Peter managed to break the last deadly link to the creature, still twitching on the bloody deck.

He was three hours away from medical attention, and bleeding profusely. Ripping the wet bandana from his neck, he bandaged the shredded finger, and began the difficult task of pulling up the anchor with one hand. Sheer adrenaline

kept him moving as he finally revved up the engines, and headed home through the treacherous shallows, well aware that if he ran aground, he was a dead man. Blood was pouring off the end of his bandaged hand. If his hull were wedged on a shoal or sandbank, he could die before the next high tide freed the boat.

Peter was not a religious man, but once he had coaxed his boat into deeper waters and was speeding home, he looked up at the smiling stars and wept. Standing at that blood-spattered center consul, and shaken to the core, he began to pray.

Death had knocked at his door before, but never quite like this. He felt overwhelmed by the fragility of each moment, the speed at which death could carry a man to the other side. As he looked over his shoulder at the shark, which lay lifeless near the engine, the magnitude of his luck swept over him like a heavy rain, pouring into the depths of his fisherman's heart.

'Thank you, God,' he whispered hoarsely, his words lifted up by the gusts of wind blowing into his face. 'Thank you.'

Sand In My Shoes

The Housekeeper's Hand

Chia loved her housekeeper, Dorothy. Sometimes she looked at the woman and thought, I love her more than my own mother.

Dorothy's hands were so big that they could wrap around a huge pumpkin, and with one quick flick of her wrists, she could easily pull the fruit off the vine. The fourth finger on her left hand was missing, and it was this physical peculiarity that often made Chia beg,

'Dorothy, tell me the story of how you lost your finger.'

She never tired of the tale, and if Dorothy did, she never showed it.

'Well child,' she would begin in her lilting Bahamian drawl, 'let me tell you how it happened. When I was a young woman and just married, my husband and I didn't have much to eat. So every day when he went to work at the saw-dust mill, and after I had finished rubbing the clothes over the old washboard and hung them up to dry, I went down to rocks by the sea. I carried some hermit crabs as bait, and threw out my fishin' line to see if I could catch us some dinner. Girl, I loved going down

there 'cause it was so peaceful, and I could get away from my mother-in-law, who was always complaining about somethin'. The other women in the village scoffed at me 'cause they thought fishin' was a man's job. But when I dangled my toes in that cool water and watched the clouds float across the sky like white angels, I felt that God was renewing my soul.'

At this point Chia usually became fidgety.

'Dorothy, just tell me the story. Don't give me a sermon now, please. I just want to know how you lost your finger!'

'Well,' Dorothy continued unruffled, 'on this day, I hadn't caught a thing. I pulled in my line but the hook caught on a piece of coral just below me. I could see the steel glinting in the sunlight under the water's surface, but no matter how hard I pulled, I just wasn't able to free it. Evenin' was comin' on and I had to get home. I didn't want to cut the line 'cause I only had a few hooks, and no money to buy more.'

'But Dorothy, hooks only cost a few pennies!' Chia cried.

'Well child, I didn't even have a few pennies, so every hook was precious to me.'

'What happened then?' asked Chia impatiently. She knew the best part of the story was just about to unfold.

'Well, I thought for a minute, and then I leaned out over the rocks and stuck my hand into the water to pry loose that stubborn hook. Now you know I have strong hands, but no matter how hard I twisted and turned, that hook was stuck. Suddenly, somethin' green and silver shot out from the ledge below me. I felt a sharp stingin' pain in my hand. Lord! I didn't know what hit me!'

'What was it?' Chia cried.

'Well child, I jerked back my hand, and there hangin' from my finger was a spotted green moray eel, and he was lookin'

me straight in the eye with no shame, whippin' his tail around my arm! Girl, I was so scared all I could do was run. I hightailed it back to the village with this creature hangin' on to me, like he owned me!'

'My friend, Annie, saw me on the path, and she cried out, "Jesus, what is this?" Then she grabbed my good arm and dragged me all the way to your Daddy's clinic, both of us screamin' like two wild hogs when they hunt them and cut them open with knives! Your Daddy, hearin' all that ruckus, stuck his head into that crowded waiting room and yelled, "For God's sake, what is all this commotion about?".'

'What did my Daddy do, Dorothy? What did he do?' cried Chia eagerly.

'Well, when he saw that spiteful moray eel hangin' from my hand, his white face turned even whiter. He yanked me into his office, and shoved my arm and that writhin' monster right on his operating table. Now let me tell you somethin' girl. Moray eels don't like to let go. That's a fact that every Bahamian fisherman knows and respects. Moray eels possess a viciousness like no other creature in the sea. They're even worse than barracudas or sharks! Your Daddy said to me, "Dorothy, we're going to have to put this slippery critter to sleep," and by God, he stuck him with a needle the size of a Coca-Cola bottle. My finger was torn to shreds. I could see white fibers that looked like the popped strings on my cousin, Ronnie's guitar. Now let me tell you, your Daddy was a calm man, and when he sewed a wound, everybody said he would concentrate jus' like God! But after some time of bein' so serious, he looked up at me and said, "I'm sorry, Dorothy. You're going to have to wear your wedding band on the other hand because I can't save this finger." After he finished

workin' on me and layin' on those clean bandages, he took his scalpel and cut open that slimy eel. Lawdy, if he didn't pull out my gold ring from that stinky belly! To tell you the truth, I should have known right then that God was giving me a sign and tryin' to tell me that my husband wasn't worthy of me wearin' his ring. But girl, that's another story that I'll keep for you when you're older!'

'What did your mother-in-law say when she saw you?' asked Chia.

'She was a nasty piece of work. All she could say was, "See Dorothy! I told you so! The Lord punished you for doin' man's work!" But in my heart, I knew that was just foolishness.'

Hazel and the Haitian

On the day that Guillaume went to find work at the village doctor's house, and first saw Hazel, he felt a thousand harvest moons rise in his chest. Hazel was not especially beautiful, but in her round, brown face, he saw a soft earnestness that made his battered soul feel like it had come home.

Guillaume was Haitian. No one knew how he had arrived on the island of Abaco in The Bahamas, and he did not speak of it to anyone. His fear ran deep through the trenches of his bowels, tying itself into tight knots that often impeded his very breath. The tremor that ran through his fine hands whenever he was faced with a new situation made him wince with shame. He hated himself for not being strong enough to control these involuntary movements; for his sensitivity to the looks on people's faces when they realized he was a foreigner. He wished that he had died in Haiti on that awful night when they had come to get him, that night which he now forced behind the veil of forgetfulness.

'What do you want?' Hazel asked as she opened the front door.

'I need a job.' Guillaume answered, painfully aware of the

way her eyes narrowed when she heard his Creole accent.

'Are you Haitian?' she asked.

'Yes, I am!' he whispered, looking straight at her.

'I don't think the Missus needs anyone,' she said, smoothing down her apron nervously.

'Please, Mademoiselle, I am so hungry.'

No one had ever called her Mademoiselle. She did not even know what the word meant, but it made her want to back away and run up the mahogany stairs into the safety of her warm kitchen. Still, something in the man's eyes held her attention, a subdued pride that did not waver in spite of the pleading in his voice.

Just then a voice called, 'Hazel, did I hear someone knocking?'

'Yes Ma'am, but it's only a Haitian looking for a job.'

'Show him up to the verandah, please. I'll be with him in a minute.'

Hazel gave Guillaume a stern glance that seemed to indicate he had better behave himself, and then turning abruptly, she mounted the stairs. Guillaume followed her. He could not help noticing the crisp neatness of the apron bow that rested on her slim waist, and the fresh scent of rain that enveloped her body. Taking a deep breath, he drank in her essence, surprised that for a moment his anxiety was not overwhelming. Holding the smoothly polished railing, he felt the trembling in his hands subside.

Hazel led him out onto the huge porch that overlooked the sparkling ocean, but she did not offer him a chair. A man like this was not fit to sit in her employer's chair. After all, he was a Haitian, and from what she knew about those people, they were low class. Just yesterday her friend Lorraine had said,

'Too many o' dees damn Haitians comin' into dis country. And gal, dey does steal from us and try take we job. If ya wan'

Sand In My Shoes

know de truth, all dey is good for is workin' in de yard or cleanin' toilets. And ya know what else? Dey is dirty. Plenty o' dem full o' diseases. Lord knows, I ain't goin' lay down wid no Haitian man! I ain't want dead.'

Hazel watched the stranger closely, afraid to leave him alone lest he steal something and she get the blame, but Guillaume just stood quietly facing the sea, his tall broad frame a lonely figure. Suddenly, she felt an unexpected twinge in her heart. The man looked so thin, and he wasn't dirty at all. Although oversized, his white shirt was spotless, and somehow when it fluttered about his body in the breeze, it gave him an air of distinction. She glanced at his face. The sun poured over his closed eyes, bringing a glow to his light brown skin, as he waited patiently, deep inside himself.

'All o' dem Haitians so black, you can't even see dem in de night!' Lorraine had said.

But this man was light skinned. As her eyes rested on his narrow facial features, she noticed his thin nose. He reminded her of her high school teacher, Mr Campbell, back in Grand Bahama. The same wide forehead and that smart look that indicated he knew about books and manners, geography and history. Mr Campbell had been adamant that his students speak the English language properly.

'Stop saying dis, dat and de udder. We're not talking about cows! Speak properly at all times. Even when you're at home or playing with your friends.'

She had listened to Mr Campbell and was proud of the way she spoke. Sometimes, when she tried to correct Lorraine, her friend would become angry, saying,

'Don't mess wid me gal, wid yo' high falutin' ways. I is a Bahamian, an' I ain't changin' de way I talk! Dat's how I is, an' dat's how I goin' stay.'

97

Now, as she watched Guillaume, it occurred to her that his English had been perfect. He had a noticeable accent, but he had not spoken pidgin English like the other Haitians she knew.

'Still, he's a Haitian,' she thought, 'something must be wrong with him!'

At that moment, the lady of the house interrupted her train of thought. Walking straight up to Guillaume, she looked him over in her authoritative way and extended her hand saying,

'Good morning, I'm Mrs Bergman. What can I do for you?'

Clasping her hand warmly, Guillaume introduced himself,

'Bon jour Madame, my name is Guillaume and I want to work. I'm not particular. I will do anything.'

Listening to the way the man pronounced his name, Hazel thought it sounded like ghee-home.

'Strange name,' she thought. 'It's so foreign. He really rolls those vowels out over his lips.'

'Guillaume,' said Mrs Bergman looking surprised, 'you speak English so well, unlike many of your fellow countrymen.'

Guillaume just nodded and said simply,

'Yes, in Haiti I was a teacher of literature and philosophy.' Then with a shy look he added, 'Madame, I hear you have a German accent, I know a few simple phrases of your language.'

'I'm worried,' said the woman, 'that you are over qualified for the work I have to offer. I can only offer you manual labour in the garden. I'm so sorry.'

'Oh, no! Please don't be sorry.' Guillaume exclaimed. 'Madame, as I said before, I'll do anything. I need to eat.' Then he added, 'My hands will do well in the earth.'

'Can you drive a car?' asked Mrs Bergman.

'Yes, of course.'

'That's great,' said Mrs Bergman, 'because often I have so

many errands to run, and when I work in the clinic with my husband, I'm just too busy. You'll be a great help to me.'

Hazel, who was watching this whole interaction, felt a thousand yellow butterflies fluttering in her stomach. Again she wanted to run away.

'Why must Mrs Bergman hire this Haitian?' she wondered angrily. 'Why can't she find a Bahamian?' But she knew the answer. Bahamians did not like gardening anymore. They felt those jobs were below them. 'Well, I'm just going to ignore him.'

'Hazel,' said Mrs Bergman, 'please bring Guillaume some breakfast and tea. After that, I will show him the garden. And make sure that you air that little house near yours. He will be staying there from now on.'

Hazel wanted to scream,

'What the devil is wrong with you, Mrs Bergman? He's a Haitian! He can't live near me! I don't care how clean or educated he is. He doesn't belong here!'

But of course she said nothing and went about her tasks, bringing out a tray with hot Johnny cake, chicken souse and lemon grass tea. In silence, she watched him eat, noticing that despite his ravenous hunger, he remained impeccably well mannered, chewing his food slowly and holding his knife and fork in the same way that her European employers did. Every now and then, a tremor would run through his hands, and she could sense his embarrassment as he struggled to stop the porcelain cup from shaking, or tried to keep the food from toppling off his fork. Something in the sensitivity of his body made her wince again. It reminded her of the time her first boyfriend had taken her to the crab pen in the back of his house. Grabbing one of the hard critters, he yanked off its claws and threw the creature back into the pen. The crab had looked so

defenseless without his arms, that Hazel had started crying.

'Hazel,' her boyfriend had said, sucking his teeth in disgust, 'dey is jus' crabs. Dey ain't got no feelins. Stop your foolishness. I know you goin' eat de crab an' rice tonight when you come to de house for dinner.'

But that night at her boyfriend's home, she refused to eat dinner, feigning a stomachache. Soon after, she broke up with him, saying she wasn't ready for a serious relationship; but the unspoken truth was that she could not imagine living with a man who tore off another creature's limbs. Secretly, she feared that in a moment of rage, he might do the same to her.

Standing there, watching Guillaume eat, she felt confused. She wanted to cry and she wanted to shout at him. Moreover, she wanted him to leave because deep inside, she had an inkling that this man was about to upset her equilibrium. And now, he had the position of gardener and chauffeur in a home, which she considered to be her realm.

'Hrrumph,' she growled to herself as she turned and headed off to make the beds, 'I'm just not going to let him get to me.'

However, she was intrigued by Guillaume. His quiet presence, the intensity in his eyes and his warm intelligence had touched her, but she did not want anything to do with him. He was from Haiti. The people who came from that island all carried a stigma. They were no good. They were ignorant, dirty and thieving, and in her mind, Guillaume was one of them. She remembered Lorraine saying,

'Gal, dem Haitians does even eat dogs. Dat ain't natural!'

Hazel could not see the walls of fear separating her from her black brothers and sisters. To her, Haitians were 'the others' and they were unacceptable. She could not conceive of the possibility that Guillaume was just as human as she was. The fact that he did

not fit the Haitian image made her even more suspicious of him.

'I hope Mrs Bergman knows what she's getting into,' she thought as she smoothed down the pillows. 'And he better not put voodoo on me or anyone in this family, or I'll have Immigration on his tail as fast as he can say hot sauce.'

***

Days passed. Guillaume loved the garden. He found solace in the hot, still air where emerald hummingbirds dived into blooming red hibiscus. His senses thrived on the feeling of soil packed hard beneath his nails, or the smell of a single allspice leaf crushed in his palm. Sometimes, he would embrace the trunk of a young madeira tree, allowing the smooth, brown bark to caress his cheek. In those rare moments, he thought of Hazel and wondered what it would be like to hold such a woman. His greatest pleasure during the day was catching a glimpse of her. Soon, he learned that she hung out the laundry at ten o'clock each morning, and as the chicken coop was nearby, he took to feeding the chickens at that time, searching for random eggs that the hens had laid during the night. From behind the fence, he could watch Hazel hang up the wash, her slender brown arms contrasting against the white sheets. He prayed for eggs because then he could give them to her when she walked past him on her way back to the house.

'Mademoiselle Hazel,' he would cry out cheerfully, 'I have some eggs for you. They're still warm!'

She would set down the empty laundry basket and open her hands to receive the fragile objects. Standing next to her, he felt the heat rise through his body. He wanted to lean over and touch his lips to her pale palms, so that she might see how he revered her. He so wanted her to look at him, but she never did. Backing away, she would simply say,

'I hope you've found them all,' and move on, those slender hips swaying like coconut fronds in the morning breeze.

Picking up the laundry basket, he would follow her to the door. Never once did she offer him a cool drink to quench his heated thirst, but instead she disappeared into the house, leaving just the familiar scent of fresh tropical rain trailing behind her.

In Haiti, women had always looked directly at Guillaume. His natural elegance and educated manner had made wooing easy for him. Women desired him and he knew it, but he was respectful, never using a woman for pure lust and then discarding her. He preferred relationships that meant something, where the giving and taking were balanced. When he was a teenager his mother said,

'Treat all women like goddesses; make them feel special, no matter what they look like or where they come from, and they will love you.'

It was advice well given and well taken, and of course, women adored him.

At university, many female students thought him a good catch, and he could have bedded any of them; yet he maintained a strict boundary, never taking advantage of the girls who studied with him. He figured that it was his position of authority that piqued their sexual interest, and therefore he remained politely aloof.

'My, how the tables have turned,' he mused, as Hazel slammed the heavy door in his face. 'In the past, there were servants to clean my home. I drank Barbancourt liqueur from fine glasses, and knew the feeling of turning women away from my bed, but look at me now: a common labourer, smelling of sweat, in a strange land where people abhor my very roots. I can't even kindle the interest of a housekeeper.'

As he went about his work in the garden, Guillaume reflected on the prejudice he was experiencing in The Bahamas. This was not about white people disliking black people. That was a common form of prejudice that everyone recognized. What he felt here, for the first time in his life, was that black people looked down on him because he was an immigrant, an outsider. Bahamian blacks saw him as inferior. Several days before, while passing a construction site in the village, a workman had called out to him,

'What you lookin' at boy? Yinna people don't live in houses in Haiti, hey?'

Guillaume had just smiled politely and walked on, fearful that any retort might lead to a fistfight.

Most white people somehow lumped all black people together, regardless of nationality or culture, but here the black Bahamians did not see Haitians as brothers originating from one Africa. Instead, Haitians were second class citizens, uneducated and destitute, and Bahamians did not want anything to do with them. The Haitian population, unable to afford proper housing, had moved to the mud flats at the edge of town where running water and sanitation services were non-existent. They lived there in hovels, barely subsisting on the meager crops they were able to grow, and unable to break the cycle of poverty that pervaded their community.

Sporadically, Immigration officers carrying weapons would raid the impoverished community, rounding up the illegal immigrants late at night, often beating them and confiscating any money they could get their hands on. Guillaume tried not to think about the awful consequences of being herded on to a boat, which would take him to Nassau for 'processing.' Jail and beatings in The Bahamas were one thing, but he knew that if he

were shipped back to Haiti, his life would end as soon as his foot touched Haitian soil. He was a political enemy, simply because he was educated. The Duvalier regime had already tried to kill him once. There would be no hesitation the second time around.

As he went about pruning and digging, he sighed, almost wishing that his cruel captors had finished him off that terrible night in Port au Prince. Guillaume was tired—tired of putting on a strong front in this strange land, and fighting the constant fear that gripped his gut and twisted him into a trembling jellyfish. He was tired of the nightmares and cold sweats, which left his bed soaking wet. And he was lonely. Since arriving in Abaco, he had not talked to anyone about his past.

'My grief and pain are stored in my heart like the milk in a ripe coconut,' he thought to himself. 'Sometimes, I feel I will break open and all of me will spill to the ground ... Mon Dieu! I must stop feeling sorry for myself and be mindful of my thoughts. I'm alive, aren't I? Yes, I'm scarred inside and out, but I still breathe. I'm still able to savour the juice of the sweet oranges in this garden, so I must be grateful.'

When a pair of wood doves fluttered in the branches above him, he looked up and whispered,

'Christ, do I ever need a woman. A companion. Someone to help me forget, and feel strong again. If only Hazel would look at me, but I don't even exist in her world.'

He did not know that Hazel was staring at him at that very moment. Standing on the verandah, hidden behind the mosquito screens, she watched his movements, her eyes lingering on his handsome profile, and the short woolly hair cropped close to his head.

Lorraine had said,

'Gal don't stand too near any o' dem Haitians cause all o'

dem got lice, and when dem Haitian lice jump on yo' head, you ain't never goin' rid yo'self o' dat plague!'

But Hazel was thinking,

'For weeks he has only ever worn the same white shirt, but it's always immaculate. He must scrub it every night against the washboard in the old iron tub. He isn't like the other Haitians who have worked here. I've never seen him bare to the waist, even in the scorching heat, and always he works like a fiend, expending all his energy digging and shoveling and lifting dead branches on to the back of that old Ford truck, never taking a break. It's like he doesn't want to think about things.'

Hazel remembered trying to tell Lorraine about Guillaume.

'He's different,' she had said. 'The other day, I watched him plant a young banana sucker in the ground. He was so gentle ... like he was talking to it with his hands, telling it to grow big and strong.'

'Gal, you so full o' shit!' Lorraine had retorted. 'Ain't nobody talks to plants. Dat boy puttin' a jinx on de plant. When you eat dem bananas, you goin' get poison!' Then scrutinizing her friend's face, she added, 'Lord, Hazel, I hope you ain't goin' soft on me!'

***

Several days later, it just so happened that Hazel was cooking a big pot of chicken souse, and she needed a dozen limes to marinate the poultry. Normally, she would have shouted for the gardener to bring her some, but she was curious about Guillaume and so she decided to go into the garden herself. The lime trees were further down the hill, away from the house, and as she ambled down the rocky path, she found herself looking into the thick foliage, trying to get a glimpse of Guillaume.

'I wonder where he is,' she thought. 'Maybe, I'll finally

catch him goofing off.'

Pushing past the many fruit trees, heavy with hog plums, oranges and grapefruits, she was about to step into a clearing when she saw him. His back was turned to her and he was crouched on his heels, furiously digging up weeds with his machete. The sound of the metal blade clicked loudly against the limestone, so he did not hear the twig snap under her feet. He did not hear the sharp intake of her breath when she saw the bare skin of his back. Thinking he was alone, Guillaume had removed his shirt. Now the sun ruthlessly exposed the deep scars and shrivelled welts that covered his torso. His brown skin was flecked with unsightly white spots in some places, and knotted into dark, painful looking bumps in others. Where the soft fat of his waist should have been, Hazel could only see ugly craters of scorched flesh. It was obvious that he had suffered horrific burns at one time in his life.

Suddenly, Hazel felt ill. It was not merely the sight of the burned flesh that turned her stomach. She had seen burns before, although not quite to the extent that Guillaume had suffered, but she was overcome with a sense of shame. Shame because she had looked upon the man with such cold judgement, while behaving in such an imperious manner. She remembered her mother saying,

'Never judge a man until you have walked a mile in his shoes.'

She turned and fled back through the trees, stopping to lean against the tall trunk of a palm tree, where she began to wretch. When the heaving stopped, she walked slowly up the hill, feeling only the emptiness of the aching void in her belly. Hazel was lonely too.

'I'm a misfit, just like Guillaume,' she reflected, her eyes wet with tears. 'I speak like a white woman, but I'm not

educated or ambitious enough to do anything great. I don't even like Lorraine, but I'm too scared to tell her because I know I'll be ostracized by everyone if I do. I want a man, but none of the guys are good enough for me. I don't like the way they talk or act. All they want to do is to prove their virility, make babies and leave. I don't belong anywhere either. I'm just a mess behind this starched apron.'

That night when Hazel went to bed, she stared at the ceiling for a long time before falling into a fitful sleep. She thought about Guillaume and wondered whether he would become a legal immigrant. While dusting the doctor's desk that morning, she had seen a copy of the application form regarding Guillaume's work permit, but she knew how long things took in The Bahamas. It could take months. Hazel had heard rumours that Immigration was on the warpath. Lorraine had laughed raucously over a cup of tea saying,

'Yeah gal! De police goin' get dem Haitian sons o' bitches soon.' Then, unable to refrain from boasting, she leaned over and whispered confidentially, 'I know cause I been sweetheartin' dat policeman, Reggie, and he tell me dey goin' raid ev'ryone soon. Not even de good doctor's house goin' be spared! Dey goin' come one night even to yo' place when nobody expectin' dem! My boyfriend tell me, he can't wait to beat up on one dem stink Haitians. He wan' use dem for a punchin' bag! Ha! Ha!'

***

Hazel woke with a start. Looking at her clock she saw it was just three in the morning. Someone was tapping at her window shutter.

'Who's there?' she called out in a frightened voice.

'Mademoiselle, please let me in, I beg of you. Please ... '

Close by, Hazel could hear voices, cursing loudly.

'God damn! We goin' catch dat fuckin' Haitian, beat his ass good, an' den send him to Fox Hill Prison. If he don't dead here, he goin' dead in dat place for sure! I hear Amnesty International identify dat as de fourth worst penitentiary in de world. Ha! Ha! Well dat's where dem frickin' Haitians belong! Dey ain't know how to live no better no how!'

Then another man said,

'Jesus Christ, Reggie! How you could let dat sucker get away? His bed was still warm!'

Swiftly, in total blackness she unlocked the door.

'Guillaume,' she whispered, 'over here.'

Guillaume crawled through the doorway on his hands and knees. As his body brushed her legs, she felt the slick wetness of cold sweat. Terror pervaded her small room.

'Hide,' she commanded. 'Hide under my bed!'

Seized by overwhelming terror herself, she began to tremble.

'What if they find him in my house?' she thought desperately. 'What will they do to me? Beat me? Throw me in prison for harbouring an illegal Haitian?'

Suddenly, she remembered the time Mrs Bergman had received an anonymous tip announcing a raid. Right after the phone call, the woman had slipped out of the house, and gone around the neighbourhood, quietly picking up several Haitians whom she proceeded to conceal in her walk-in closet. Then, she had locked the German Shepherd in her bedroom. Of course, the dog had gone wild barking, with only a door between himself and the Haitians. When the police arrived, they asked if they could search the house.

'Sure,' she had said haughtily, pretending to be insulted. 'But you enter my bedroom at your own risk. My dog does not cherish intruders. By the way, he is trained to attack.'

Hazel, who did not understand why Mrs Bergman had placed herself at risk for a few dirty Haitians, was nevertheless impressed with her brazen attitude, and when she commented on it after the police were gone, Mrs Bergman had simply smiled saying,

'Of course I was nervous but I wasn't going to let them know. Furthermore, it's a well-known fact that Bahamians are scared to death of dogs, so those poor Haitians were safe. At least for today.'

Now it was time for Hazel to summon her own bravado.

'I can't believe I've put myself in this position for a Haitian! What on earth has come over me?'

But already she was throwing on her dressing gown and resolving to pull herself together.

'Open up or we goin' break down dis door!' a man shouted, banging loudly. Feigning sleepiness, Hazel unlatched the door and rubbed her eyes.

'What's wrong? Has something happened?' she asked. Three men, all dressed in green khakis, were pointing guns straight at her.

'Any Haitians in here?' questioned the first officer in a menacing voice, while trying to push her aside. But Hazel stood firm, praying that he would not smell the fear oozing from her pores. Steely-eyed she retorted,

'I am a Bahamian citizen and you better show me a search warrant, or I'll press charges on your backsides as fast as you can blink your eyes! You hear me? And I'm not joking!' Then, as though disgusted with their total lack of discernment, she added, 'And besides, do I look like a woman who would have a Haitian sleeping in my bed?'

The men looked at each other and the leader responded sheepishly,

'No, dat's true. You don't look like no whore! You look too pretty to be lovin' up on some ugly Haitian.' Stepping closer, he asked, 'Ain't you Lorraine's friend?'

Hazel nodded.

Then to the others, 'Let's go boys. We is jus' wastin' time here. Maybe we'll find de son-of-a-bitch hidin' in de bushes. I jus' feel like givin' somebody a good cut-ass tonight.'

Hazel watched the men disappear into the blackness.

'You can come out now, Guillaume,' she said softly. The adrenaline racing through her body made her hands shake, and she could barely strike the match to light the kerosene lamp. In the darkness, she felt his hands touch her own. He was shaking too, awful tremors passing through his fingertips. Taking the matches from her hand, he dropped them on the table.

'Thank you, Mademoiselle Hazel. You saved my life. I will be forever in your debt.' Then, whispering, 'Perhaps it is not wise to light the lamp now. They may still be nearby.'

But Hazel, who knew that the danger had passed, blurted out, 'You don't want me to see you because your body is so badly scarred. Am I right?'

Guillaume did not respond. All Hazel heard was the sound of his breath catching in his throat.

'I saw you working in the garden,' she continued, 'near the fruit trees. You didn't notice me, but I saw you without your shirt.'

Silence.

'What happened to you?' she queried. Then softly, 'My God, you must have suffered.'

Guillaume feared an internal dam would burst if he opened his mouth to speak. The terror of the last moments still vibrated in his head, but that had not nearly as much power

as the pictures of torture that ravaged his mind.

'I ... I ... don't....' he stammered.

'Tell me, please,' she urged, 'I want to know.'

In the darkness of the room, Guillaume felt dizzy. Leaning his elbows on the wooden table, he held his head between his hands, as if by this gesture he could control the onslaught of images eating at his brain. He was afraid that if he gave them a voice, they would devour him forever. He saw himself being fried, broiled and stripped raw, only to be chewed and spit out by demons.

'No woman will want your body any more!' the demons screamed. 'It will turn her stomach to run her hands over your skin. Ugly holes and hollow pits! No smoothness left. No more velvet in the night. Only the jagged shell of a crushed crawfish left to burn in the coals!'

Hazel waited, her silence engulfing him like a womb. Sensing his despair, she felt helpless, but the stillness was precisely what Guillaume needed to revisit his terrifying past, and touch the unspeakable trauma of nearly dying at the hands of human beings turned vicious. As they sat together in the darkness, her simple presence was the container for his terror. He needed another human being to be with him, or he would have fallen into a hell from which there was no return.

He heard the sound of her fingers sliding across the table, but she did not try to touch him. His skin felt dry now, hot with a feverish glow, as the agonizing pictures came closer.

'Tell me,' she whispered.

Taking a deep breath, he began,

'My story is not unique. Many have known the agony of torture. I differ only in that I am one of the few who survived.' He paused before continuing. 'Hazel, have you ever heard of

the Ton Ton Macoutes?'

'No,' answered Hazel hoarsely, aware that he had not prefaced her name with Mademoiselle.

'The Ton Ton Macoutes is a vicious guard of men who control the Haitian people for Papa Doc. You know who he is?'

'Yes,' Hazel replied. 'I have heard of him. He is the leader of your country.'

'Well,' said Guillaume, 'he's not a leader, but a dictator. A tyrant, who disposes of anyone whom he feels poses a threat to his regime. He is a coward, and he uses the Ton Ton Macoutes, or Bogeymen as they are called, to do his dirty work.'

Guillaume paused, and she could sense his uncertainty.

'What happened?' she asked, urging him on.

'When they came for me in the middle of the night, they were wearing boots and carrying clubs and machetes. They were men like me, but everyone was afraid of them because they killed for no reason. They killed if they had only a silly reason. They killed just for the sake of killing. They smashed in the front door of my home. They smashed my furniture and burned my books outside. They pulled my mother from her bed and.... '

His voice faltered.

'What did they do to her,' Hazel asked, straining to see his face in the dark.

'They tied me to the foot of her bed and made me watch as they violated her. Then they used a machete and pierced the womb that held me. She died in a sea of blood.'

Hazel thought she would be sick again. Instead, she swallowed the salty taste in her mouth and fought back the nausea.

'They dragged me naked to the police station, where they beat my hands and the soles of my feet with spiked clubs and forced my head into buckets of piss.'

'Why did they do this to you?' cried Hazel.

'They told me I was a traitor because I was friendly with a man named Hector, who was wanted for secretly planning an uprising against Papa Doc. When I explained that I knew he lived on the same street, but that I had not seen him in months, they beat me again and called me a liar. They demanded to know where he was, but I couldn't tell them. Honestly, I could not.'

'What happened then?' asked Hazel.

'Perhaps they really thought I had information because after that, they took me to Duvalier's palace. I waited for hours in a room. I was not allowed to use the toilet, and finally Papa Doc himself came in. I cannot forget him, because he was eating Fois Gras from a silver plate with his bare fingers.'

'What is Fois Gras?' asked Hazel uncertainly.

'It's an expensive, imported pâté made of duck or chicken liver. All of Haiti would die to eat something like that. The people are starving. Many of them are just skin and bones! The only people who have any money are those who support Francois Duvalier and his monstrous regime. Anyway, Duvalier looked at me and said,

"What have we here? A mulatto? You should have more breeding, you elitist pig, but you stink! You smell of piss! Now I can't even eat my food because you make me sick!" and he threw the pâté at my head. Then staring at my face, he asked me to tell him the whereabouts of Hector Riobe. He said that he knew I was friendly with Riobe, and that was dangerous because Riobe was a rebel planning to overthrow him. When I could not give him the information he wanted, he turned to the Ton Ton leader and said, "Take the filthy bugger away!"

"What shall we do with him?" the leader asked.

"Burn him! He will ignite nicely with grease on his body."

Hazel felt her heart racing. In her world, such violence was unthinkable.

'They tied my hands and feet, and took me to the edge of a cornfield where they poured gasoline over my body. I don't know why they didn't douse my face. Maybe, they wanted me to see the flames burning me alive. One of them struck a match, and that was it. They jumped in their car and sped away.'

'Oh my Lord!' said Hazel, shaking her head in disbelief. 'How did you manage to survive?'

'There was a little chapel just down the road. The priest saw the car stop, and following his God given intuition, he crept through the corn. He waited until they disappeared, and then tearing off his robe, he smothered the flames that consumed me. That good man carried me back to his home and cared for my burns, washing me, feeding me, and soothing me with prayers. I wished time and time again that he had let me die, for although he was a man of mercy, my pain was merciless.'

For a long while, Hazel could not speak. She was flooded with remorse, and the awareness of her previous coldness towards the man weighed heavily on her heart.

'I'm sorry,' she said, 'I have been so unkind, so ignorant.'

'Mademoiselle Hazel…. '

'Please,' she interrupted, 'don't call me Mademoiselle. I don't know what it means, but it feels like you place me on a pedestal with that title. I … I … don't feel comfortable.'

Guillaume nodded. He understood.

'But Hazel, you saved my life. No greater gift can be given. You are a courageous woman.'

'How did you make it to The Bahamas?' she asked, embarrassed at his compliment.

'On a dinghy, carrying twenty Haitian refugees. It was overloaded and capsized in the Whale Cay Channel. Only six of us survived. I was able to help a woman carrying an infant. So you see, I am blessed to have been able to repay God.'

***

Dawn was breaking. Violet ribbons streaked the sky and shimmers of gold filtered through the curtains. It was Sunday. Outside an occasional cricket still chirped, holding onto the night before, creeping into a tree crevice, while in the distance, a rooster was determined to rouse the world.

Hazel observed the man before her, making sure to keep her eyes on his face. She had a sudden notion that he would leave if he caught her looking at his scars. And she did not want him to go. Although his story had left her feeling raw, his company was the balm that eased her discomfort. She felt drawn to his soft-spoken demeanor, his warm eyes and the way he still smiled at life's adversities, but she was shy and filled with apprehension. Her nerves tingled.

She rose to make some tea. Setting the steaming mug on the table, she noticed the awful tremor in his hand as he reached to grasp it.

'I ... I'm so sorry,' he stammered self consciously as some of the liquid spilled on the table. 'I ... I have no control over it. Ever since that night ... whenever I feel anxious or touch something hot, I ... I ... tremble. I hate it!'

'Are you anxious right now?' asked Hazel.

Guillaume nodded.

'It has been many moons since I talked with a woman, and I'm afraid that....'

'That I will be disgusted by the scars your body bears.'

'Yes,' Guillaume conceded, looking away, 'but it would be

worse to see pity.'

After a while, Hazel asked,

'What was the worst part of your ordeal? Was it the pain? Was it your mother?'

Guillaume answered slowly, 'No, those things were terrible, but what I dreaded most were the looks in my tormentors' eyes, the coldness that refused to see my suffering, the icy numbness that separated them from me and refused to see me as another human being. Their eyes will haunt me until I die.'

Hazel, who suddenly felt that her heart was burning like the rising sun outside her window, could not stop herself from reaching out to stroke his scarred shoulder. Inside her, waves were breaking over unknown shores. She could not explain it, but she wanted to swim deep into the intelligence he exuded. It was not his body that moved her, but something else, something invisible. It made her feel more alive than ever before. She had never known a man like him. In his presence, she felt changed. There was so much she wanted to ask him, and instinctively she knew he would answer with wisdom and honesty. He captivated her and this shook her sense of self, because he was certainly not the man on whom she would have spent her fantasies. Still, she sensed his greatness and she wanted to merge with that. So, when they both stood up wordlessly and embraced each other, there was no hesitation. Guillaume felt a thousand harvest moons in his hands, and Hazel thought she could hear the sun singing hymns of light.

They lay together for a long time, infusing each other with the silence that belongs to new lovers. The skin of her hands was surprisingly soft, and when her fingers moved over the hideous scars that covered his body, Guillaume wept.

In turn, Guillaume bathed her body in a tenderness that was almost excruciating.

'How could this man care so much for me?' she wondered between breaths of pleasure. Her rapture came in waves of yearning for that which she had never known, and the acknowledgment of this longing made Hazel weep too.

Hours later, when the heat of the morning lay like a heavy net over the lovers, they fell into a deep sleep. Holding Hazel close, Guillaume dreamed of soft, colourful silks fluttering in tropical breezes. Outside the window, flies were buzzing and hitting the screens, impatiently trying to get into the house.

Hazel did not know how long she slept, but suddenly she was awakened by a high pitched, cackling voice.

'Jesus! Lord have mercy! What is dis? Hazel, what de hell you doin' sleepin' wid dis man?'

Sitting straight up in bed, her breasts bare, Hazel stared at Lorraine, who was standing at the foot of her bed wearing a gaudy red dress, ready to go to church. Hazel had forgotten about going to church with her friend, just as she had forgotten that Lorraine had a key to her front door.

'Gal, I was callin' yo' name and when you ain't answer me, I was tinkin' sumptin' happen to you, so I come inside. But I ain't never thought you was in here wid dis Haitian! You gone crazy hey?'

Sucking her teeth, she turned her head and spit on the floor in disgust, while the brim of her large felt hat flopped with righteous indignation.

'Gal, you is goin' straight to hell! God don't like ugly you know! Here you is right in front o' my eyes, wrappin' yo'self around dis stink man!' Then taking a closer look at Guillaume she cried, 'And he all scorch up! His skin look like one curly tail lizard. How you could rub on him, gal?'

Guillaume, who was sitting up now, tried to cover himself

with the sheet while Lorraine started beating his feet with her straw bag.

'Get your hip from round here!' she yelled. 'You mussee put voodoo on dat woman for her to want spend de night wid you!'

Hazel, who had been rendered speechless by the intrusion that had shattered her reverie, suddenly sprang from the bed, baring her teeth like a tiger. Her naked body was taut with fury as she shouted at Lorraine,

'How dare you enter my house and invade my privacy with your wretched nastiness! Get out!'

But Lorraine spun around, perspiration flushing her cheeks.

'You stop talkin' to me in dat fine English manner you tink is so holy! You ain't nuttin' gal! Ain't you still servin' white folk?'

With one swift movement, she slapped Hazel hard across the face.

'You is jus' a no good for nuttin bitch! You should be shame to call yo'self a Bahamian! You ain't even know who you is! You is a black whore tryin' to be white, grindin' a Haitian.'

Afraid that Lorraine would strike Hazel again, Guillaume moved to protect her, but Hazel motioned for him to stay where he was. Her eyes were riveted on Lorraine's. What she saw was both deeply disturbing and fascinating. Never had she been the object of such hatred. As she gazed at the woman she once called her friend, she was met with a coldness that would have killed if it were given free rein.

In that instant, Hazel clearly saw that Lorraine despised her for being different, for speaking English properly. Lorraine hated her for opening her heart to a foreigner. It made no difference that Guillaume was a black man. He was an outsider. It did not matter that he was a human being. In Lorraine's eyes, he was a savage.

'But Lorraine!' cried Hazel in a wild attempt to make her

friend understand, 'he's flesh and blood just like you and me! He has feelings! His heart beats just like any man's!'

Throwing her a scornful look, Lorraine sneered,

'Dat's a Haitian, dat ain't no man!' With those words she grimaced contemptuously and stormed out of the house, leaving Hazel and Guillaume in stunned silence.

'Ma cherie' said Guillaume, 'I am sorry that I have placed you in this compromising situation! It might be better if I leave.'

'No,' replied Hazel, 'don't say that.' Turning to him, her eyes were sad but wise. 'All my life I have been afraid that I did not belong. I have acted in ways that went against the grain of my conscience, listening to people like Lorraine, simply because exclusion felt like death.' Then laughing softly she added, 'I feel like I've been run through a hundred washing machines ... I am exhausted but I feel so clean, as though the fabric of my body were transparent, light, free. This is what you have given me, and all this in one night.'

Smiling at him she continued, 'I don't know what God has in store for us, but let's make this bed our sanctuary today.'

As she lay there in the stark daylight with Guillaume's arms around her, Hazel felt that a missing part of herself had been returned to her. She did not want to lose the feeling of wholeness ever again.

'Tonight, we will go to Mrs Bergman. She will hide you.'

That evening at sundown, they knocked on the doctor's front door, each of them remembering their first encounter. When Mrs Bergman answered the door, she smiled,

'What can I do for you? It's Sunday, there's no work today.'

Hazel spoke.

'There was a raid last night. Guillaume hid at my house, but Lorraine found out this morning ... so I'm sure they

know. Mrs Bergman, can you hide….'

Without waiting for Hazel to finish Mrs Bergman said,

'Guillaume, I'm sorry you had to spend the night in fear. Your work permit came through late Friday afternoon, but you had already gone, so I couldn't tell you. You're legal now.'

Then, noticing how close the two were standing, a twinkle came into her eyes and she added, 'Of course, if you two were married, Guillaume could remain in The Bahamas forever.'

The word 'married' sent Hazel's mind reeling.

'Mrs Bergman,' she whispered, 'I don't know if I'm ready for that. I mean….'

'Hazel, I'm just joking.'

But something in the white woman's eyes was direct. She seemed to be looking straight into Hazel's heart.

Quietly, she continued,

'The heart has a way of overcoming life's cruelest and most difficult challenges. One day, I will tell you some stories about my past and about Germany, the country I was forced to leave because of a hatred so great that millions of people were killed. Murdered because they were Jews. It is a tragic thing, but people often hate those who are different. We have not yet learned as human beings to honour and enjoy our differences, simply because we are afraid of them. Anyone who is different threatens the core of our existence. That fear makes people do bad things.'

A faraway look clouded the woman's eyes, and both Hazel and Guillaume could sense her sadness. As she watched Mrs Bergman, it dawned on Hazel that hatred and prejudice could happen between all people. It was not just a matter of colour, nationality, education or wealth. People hated each other for so many reasons. In Mrs Bergman's case, white people in

Germany had killed Jews, who were white too, just because they had a different culture. It was a crushing realization, and she felt overwhelmed.

As if reading Hazel's thoughts, Mrs Bergman went on,

'But the heart can accomplish things of lasting significance, because it has the power to dissolve fear. That's why we must listen to it and trust its' deepest messages. Only love can impel us to work in the service of something that is greater than ourselves. And only love can embrace both the cruel and the kind. It is up to each one of us to make this world a place where everyone belongs. Many of us are called to this task in different ways.'

Suddenly, she smiled brightly and looking at them both, she exclaimed,

'Come on you two! Here I am rambling on, and I can see that you are both exhausted. Let's have a glass of wine and drink to life, and to all that has gone before and all that is yet to come.'

As they sat on the porch, Hazel thought about the events of the past twenty-four hours. Instinctively she knew that something greater was calling her and wanting to use her for a purpose. It frightened her, but at the same time it gave her strength. Turning to look at Guillaume, she felt her life was at a new starting point, not necessarily a comfortable one but one that held the potential for love.

Tenderly, Guillaume reached for her hand, the trembling in his fingers faint, but present like the ripples on the sea created by the underlying currents. She did not know where fate would take them, but she felt humbled and somehow in tune with the unknown.

Together they watched the fiery sun dip into the purple ocean, while on the horizon a pregnant harvest moon intent on kissing the stars rolled slowly toward heaven.

Moonbeams & Mystery

Moonlight and Margaritas

Once there was an island girl who searched for the meaning of life. She wished to be on a path that would unveil the mysteries of the sands beneath her feet and the swirling oceans teeming with hidden life. Sometimes, in rare moments of joy, when she watched a dolphin spinning into thin air or a pelican swooping low to touch the sea, she could feel a glimmer of hope. At times when her meditations led her to glimpse the timeless world she thought,

'Maybe now I can understand the Mystery of Life!'

But the feeling lasted only for a short time, before she reflected again,

'No! There must be an even better path.'

So for years, she went to seminars and schools in distant countries, hoping to find a master who might point her in the right direction. She learned many things, but the ultimate path still eluded her.

One evening, after she had returned to the island from one of her trips, she was sitting in a local bar by the ocean, drinking a glass of wine, when an old man sat down on the

bar stool beside her. His eyes gleamed at her strangely. At first she thought,

'Oh no! He's coming on to me!' but when she looked into his eyes something indescribable caught her attention. His irises were opaque, nearly transparent, twinkling with laughter and yet something holy and mysterious lived within the doorways to his soul.

He ordered a margarita. Secretly, she laughed to herself, 'I hope he knows how strong they are here!'

Suddenly, he turned to her and asked,

'What closes your heart?'

Normally, the woman would have been shocked. Well, she was for a moment, but then she felt an overwhelming desire to talk to the white-haired man.

'Uh,' she stammered, 'I ... I need to think about that.'

'I have time,' he said, looking at the full glass of margarita. And then he repeated the question, 'What closes your heart?'

Surprised, the woman noticed that words began to cascade from her mouth, and she could not silence her tongue.

'Sometimes, I feel I could be so much more, but a mean voice tells me I'm not creative enough. I want to write a book, but I'm afraid that I can't get the ideas together and that my creativity is a desert with no oasis.

'My heart shuts down when my lover doesn't clean the kitchen, or when he leaves a trail of clothes on the floor. It shuts down again because I feel I should rise above all these mundane things.

'I yell at him, and then I feel that I am not sexy enough and he'll leave me. I get angry at silly things, and to make things worse, I get angry at my anger and even that pisses me off!'

Momentarily embarrassed, she murmured, 'Please excuse my language.'

The old man just smiled, as if inviting her to continue. The woman closed her eyes. When she opened them she said,

'I have studied the way energy flows through the human body, and I think I'm a healer, but I wonder if anything I do helps anyone. I'm frightened of being a fraud in God's eyes, or anyone else's for that matter. I've been searching for years, but the answers always seem to be somewhere else, somewhere outside of me, never where I am. I feel so utterly human.'

Straightening her spine, she tried to appear calm and said,

'Let me see if I can distill all my ramblings down to something that makes sense.'

Again, he just smiled while she continued,

'I think fear closes my heart. Yes, I'm afraid. You see, I don't really trust life. I don't trust others. I don't trust myself, and in spite of all the places I've gone to find Him, God is still somewhere totally in outer space, so I don't trust Him!'

Then, placing her hand on her heart, she exclaimed,

'But I have such burning in here! I have such a burning that I feel I'm on fire!'

Suddenly, quite involuntarily, her eyes filled with tears.

'Damn!' she thought to herself, 'I can't believe I'm crying. What's this old man going to think of me?'

Still he said nothing, but reaching out, he took hold of her hand. She could feel the little grains of salt where his fingertips had touched the rim of his glass. Mortified, she wondered if everyone around her would think she was dating the old man, but his hand felt safe. It demanded nothing from her.

Turning, she stared at him, her heart skipping like pilchards over the water. Streams of light flowed between them, touching everyone else in the room, even those people she didn't like.

'Listen,' he said gently, 'when you desire something, you

want to move toward it like a child that wants to move toward love and safety but cannot, because of certain unfortunate circumstances. Love that is interrupted turns to pain. It becomes too much to feel. Later in life, this pain feels like anger and despair. But it is still a form of love. When we reconnect to love, we heal the interruption. When we can accept what is and what has been without resisting and struggling, then we can find peace and life seems to fall into place.'

The woman thought of those she loved so deeply, her dead parents and her brother, who had killed himself. Remembering the many times she had been cruel to others and herself, she felt ashamed. Distraught, she averted her eyes, but the old man's voice commanded,

'Look at me! If you turn away from my eyes for fear of judgement, you also turn away from finding acceptance and love.'

Again she gazed at him, sensing mysteries beyond mysteries of life, death and worlds unknown. She could hardly bear the intensity of the moment, but always he kept bringing her back, silently urging her to surrender.

Her mind wobbled as she whispered, 'What is the truth?'

The old man did not answer, but even as she asked the question, peace flooded her heart.

From beneath fluttering eyelids, she watched him become a membrane of light through which the source flowed freely. Finally, he spoke,

'Truth is whatever serves and enhances life. If you pay attention, you can feel the truth right away. It opens your heart. Your body responds with liveliness. If it is not the truth, your body becomes hard and heavy.'

The woman rested her head on the bar counter so she could be more comfortable. Through the door, she could see moon-

light caressing the foaming waves. Nothing else mattered. For what seemed an eternity, she stayed there looking at the ocean and the old man. No words passed between them, and yet everything was known. Not once did he make an overt gesture. Trust flowed through her like a river. Never had she known such safety, such acceptance.

He did not try to influence her, and yet she was aware that the magnitude of their fleeting intimacy had changed her forever.

Occasionally, her thoughts contracted, driving imperceptible tremors of doubt through her body. When this happened, he soothed her and stroked her hair with his fingers.

'He is like a father,' she thought. 'No! He is like The Father.'

She knew she was linked to something far greater than anything words could express. This force was reconnecting her to everything, to God, to life, to herself—into generations past and future. In the presence of this power, everything melted—her phobias and hurts, her fears and self doubt.

There she lay, utterly content. Suddenly, a giggle rose from the bottom of her belly, while simultaneously, tears dripped off the end of her nose mingling with the coarse salt and condensation from his glass.

Right there, in that noisy bar on her own island, she saw the Face of Love. A deep stirring moved in her being, and without doing anything, she understood that she herself was one of the many faces.

After a long while, she sat up.

The old man excused himself. He did not return, and she did not look for him. His work was the work of the soul, and his time with her was over.

In awe, she stared at the light sparkling in the shards of his icy margarita while she herself felt drunk on bliss and gratitude.

The Touch of Spirit

The touch of spirit on my body is the most desirable kiss,
Though transient and rarely encountered, it is never forgotten.
It wafts through my senses bearing the fragrance of roses eternal,
Reminding me of all that is holy.

The touch of spirit on my body flows through my veins
In purple rivers of ancient wine.
When first I sipped this elixir, I fell deeply into trance,
Far away from the drunken crowd,
Far away from earthly desires which drive me blindly forward.

In an instant, I knew that I was home.
In an instant, I did not fear death or living.
Instead, I wanted to be steeped in sweet forgetfulness
Remembering only that which has true meaning.

The touch of spirit on my body has penetrated my skin
And with this piercing comes a longing so intense,
That I cry out His sacred name, begging to be wrapped once more,
In that which is invisible, but contains me nonetheless.

The touch of spirit on my body is the velvet night
Into which I wantonly surrender,
And all that I think I am, dissolves,
Each fragment shattering, every habitual form shifting,
And as my ego dwindles into nothing,
I am miraculously unafraid.

The touch of spirit on my body has liberated my spirit,
Opening my heart to the fleeting taste of freedom,
Bubbling and boiling at the core of my silence,
Infusing me with a peace that reaches far beyond my understanding.

I want to grasp it, hold it close
So that it never leaves me, but already it is gone,
Evaporating like crystal drops of water on dry, thirsty ground.
I walk on, my feet heavy on the earthen path.
Ah, but I have known the touch of spirit on my body,
And though the kiss may fade, the memory lingers sweetly.

The Yellow Balloon

Cordelia and John had desired a child for years, but time was passing them by like the rushing tides under the bridge that Cordelia crossed every day on her way to the straw market. Often she would stop and look down at the turbulent blue water of the Atlantic, her eyes wistful.

Whenever she felt particularly optimistic, she would run to the bridge and cast a precious penny into the crashing waves, praying with a fervour akin to madness, for God to open her womb and allow a child to root itself into the depths of her body.

At other times, she was overcome with such longing that she felt her skin would crack open with grief if she were never to feel a baby's hand caressing her cheek. The sadness made her legs as heavy as the burlap sacks full of mangoes and bananas that she toted to the market. She thought her limbs would crumble to dust if she were not allowed to run after a child and scoop it up in her arms.

At night, although completely exhausted, she would touch her husband's hard muscular belly, stroking him until the passion mounted in his loins and she could feel him enter

her. She waited only for the sacred moment of his release, each time crying out her silent prayer. *Fill me! Oh living God, fill me!*

Often, when John was worn tired by the day's work and fell asleep wearing his dusty boots, she would not let him rest but arouse his manhood, coaxing from him the liquid which felt more precious to her than gold. Cordelia was not lewd in any way, but simply driven by an unwavering desire to be heavy with child. For her, the sexual act was holy because it nourished her hope.

At the same time, she was terrified that if she missed one night, she would miss the child. God's portal of opportunity would close. The fear gnawed at her belly like the rats that chewed on the corn stored in the old wooden bin behind the house. Over and over she heard the silent words: *If only I could have a child, I would be at peace. If only I could have a child, I would be happy.*

Each year she watched the sows bearing down to birth their piglets. When her donkey was pregnant, Cordelia steadied the beast and supported the struggling foal in her arms before it fell to the ground. She did not care that her clothes were soaked in blood. Little chicks in need of warmth found a haven in her hands. She would let nothing die if it were young. She loved anything that was helpless and innocent.

She pleaded with God, bargained with Him, but to no avail. At times, her heart would fill with such bitterness that she would rage at Him, cursing her infertility. This rage was soon followed by shameful remorse, and she would run to the bridge with frangipani flowers in her hand. Throwing the golden petals into the swirling ocean, she begged to be forgiven.

One day, after such an episode, she found herself leaning on the railing of the rickety bridge, her hot tears falling into

the azure sea below. Turning her head, she saw an old woman sitting on the boulders below, holding what appeared to be a light, yellow ball attached to a fine string. She rubbed her swollen eyes to make sure that the woman was real. The woman smiled and beckoned her to come down and sit on the cool rocks beside her. Picking her way down the slippery embankment, Cordelia felt the thorny bougainvillea bushes scratching her legs, yet she hurried on. She had a strange feeling that the old woman might disappear.

Cordelia knew everyone in the nearby villages, but this woman had never before crossed her path. For a moment, Cordelia thought the woman resembled the wooden statue of the fertility goddess which she kept hidden under her bed. She had paid the obeah woman dearly for the statue. However, a closer look at the old woman's face revealed pale wrinkled skin, very different from Cordelia's, which gleamed liked wild coffee beans in the sun.

'My child,' said the wizened woman, 'your pain is so great that even the ocean swells with your tears. Why do you cry?'

'Oh Mother,' Cordelia replied, her tears falling like shining dewdrops, 'I long for my womb to bear fruit. More than anything, I want to hold a baby in my arms, but I am barren.'

The old woman remained silent for quite some time, her eyes closed, an expression of deep reflection on her wise face. Cordelia waited, as she knew she must, watching the yellow ball float like a feather at the end of the string held in the pale, veined hand. Many minutes passed and still the crone sat in silence; the only audible sounds were the rasping of her breath and the ocean drawing itself into the depths.

A ring gleamed on her finger in the sunlight; purple sparks flashing from the stone, as the bobbing ball initiated tiny

movements. Turning, she looked at Cordelia, a strange, golden light emanating from her eyes. At first, sky blue, they now glowed yellow, like the rare candles Cordelia lit in church when she prayed for a baby.

Cordelia trembled because the power streaming from those strange eyes created a searing heat in her womb and belly.

'Have no fear, my daughter,' whispered the woman, 'I will not hurt you. Your wish has great power. You will be with child soon. However, you must remember that your greatest happiness may also be your greatest sorrow.'

Cordelia, who was overcome with great joy, was suddenly afraid her heart would burst.

'Thank you!' she cried. 'Thank you!'

The wise woman's eyes filled with compassion before she spoke.

'Look at this thing I am holding. It is called a balloon. If I release it, it will fly high into the heavens, way beyond the clouds. But if I hold it, it cannot make the journey. At some point, it will lose its breath and fall withered to the ground.'

'Where did you get this from?' asked Cordelia curiously.

'In the city where I come from, there are many children with balloons. They are often used for birthday celebrations.'

'What a fine object.' remarked Cordelia. 'If I have a child, I will buy many of these for him.'

The old woman simply nodded and handed Cordelia the string.

'Let it go,' she said.

'No! I want to keep it!'

'Let it go,' repeated the old woman gently. 'Watch it as it soars.'

Cordelia opened her hand, and the balloon flew up into the

sky, giving Cordelia such pleasure that she herself laughed like a child.

'Go home now,' the old woman urged, 'and wait until your husband chooses to make love to you. Then give yourself with wild abandon, fly free over the sugar cane fields, and surrender yourself to the waves of the sea.'

Cordelia kissed the aging hands and ran home to John. The old woman watched her leave and bowed her head to pray.

Several days later, Cordelia and John made love. Their desire for each other flowed like the rising tide, and Cordelia did not demand his essence, but received him with great love and openness of spirit.

The next moon came and Cordelia was with child. Delighted, she ran through the forests and splashed in the turquoise waters which caressed the shores near her home. When the sun was high, she would visit John in the fields. He would see her in the distance, carrying a basket filled with tasty morsels of food. There, on that fertile soil, they would sit while Cordelia fed him conch fritters and chunks of juicy watermelon. Using mint leaves, she would wipe the sweat away from his brow with her slender fingers. John saw that she was radiant and he rejoiced.

Within a year, a beautiful boy was born. His skin was mahogany brown and his hair the colour of golden corn. The village people thought he possessed magical powers because his hair was such an odd colour. It seemed to frame his face in an ever-present glow.

Cordelia was happy. She felt full, and no longer cried or demanded anything of God. She was a wonderful mother, carrying her boy everywhere in her arms. When she worked, she strapped him to her strong shoulders, never leaving him alone. Not once did she complain that he was heavy.

Cordelia's and John's lives were filled with pleasure. Their son, so intelligent, was able to speak with confidence at an early age. Running around the hut with naked legs, he would help his mother with chores, or roll in the grass with the dogs and goats. There was no fear in him, for he had known only love.

Before his fifth birthday, Cordelia and John decided to take him on the mail-boat to the city of Nassau. They wanted to buy gifts, clothes and toys, whatever they could afford, so that he too, could have pleasure, in return for all the laughter he had brought them. Once there, Cordelia shopped with enthusiasm, packing all the presents in a special bag that she had woven from colourful straw.

The day of the celebration arrived. They had decided to stay in Nassau with Cordelia's sister who lived there. Cordelia prepared a mild chicken curry with tasty biscuits and baked crabs. Cookies made from sesame seeds, sweetened with honey, were piled high on a wooden plate.

A large yellow balloon purchased for the occasion was tied to a long ribbon, which hung to the floor. When her son came into the room dressed in a pure white shirt and soft, cotton trousers, Cordelia was so proud she wanted to cry.

Laughing gaily, the boy grasped the ribbon, pulling at the balloon with wonder until it was next to his face. His green eyes flashed with pleasure as his arms circled the bobbing ball.

'Mama look,' he cried 'I can dance!' and he whirled around the room like a dervish, hopping and skipping until he was completely breathless.

Suddenly, a loud popping sound pierced the air, and the boy inhaled sharply. Cordelia jumped, feeling an unknown terror surge through her body. Her son fell backwards, his face ashen, his lips the colour of purple scarlet plums. She screamed and

called his name, hugging and shaking him, but he did not respond. There was only silence, broken by the faint, wheezing sound of thin rubber fluttering against his windpipe when he gasped for air. Cordelia's sister wasted no time.

'Come Cordelia! Come John!' she yelled. 'The hospital is around the corner. We must get him there quickly!'

Barefooted, they ran like wildfire through the dirty streets, with Cordelia crying and praying for God to save her baby.

***

The men in white were kind, but their eyes held a look of resignation. She knew they were afraid to talk to her. Her son lay on the crisp, white sheets, his brown body turning yellow under the fluorescent lighting. Needles bruised his smooth arms and his skin became so translucent that Cordelia thought she could see his eyes shining beneath the dark lashes. But never once did they open. He seemed poised between two worlds.

'Do not leave me my sweet one,' she wept as she clasped his small hand. Her will felt as mighty as the ocean swells in the Atlantic. The kind nurses tried to support her trembling shoulders, but she shook them off.

'I cannot let him go! I will not let him go!'

One night, wanting to splash water on her flushed face, she went to the bathroom down the hall. Passing an open door, she saw an old woman lying on the hospital bed. The woman was motioning for Cordelia to come in and sit on the white sheets. The window was open; a cool jasmine scented breeze touched Cordelia's skin. Cordelia recognized the old woman at once.

'Why?' she cried, 'Why are you taking him from me? I cannot let him go. I love him too much. It's not fair that you should take him back! He is mine!'

The old woman smiled weakly and answered,

'It is not I who takes him from you, my dear. I have waited so that I may join him on this part of his journey. The time he spent with you was a gift, but he belongs elsewhere. Do you remember the balloon? You let it fly and laughed with pleasure when it disappeared into the heavens. Now, you must let your boy go with grace.'

Cordelia choked on her tears, as the woman continued,

'Your son dances between this world and the next, but he cannot cross the veil if your will holds him back. You see, sweet woman, he loves you too much.'

Cordelia nodded, deep sobs wracking her body, her stomach knotting in pain as she looked at the distant stars. So much love, so much pain.

The old woman stretched out her thin arms, drawing Cordelia to her breast. Stroking her hair, she whispered,

'My daughter, the bonds of love can never be broken. They last forever, wrapping our hearts with ribbons of infinite tenderness. Love cannot die. Your son will always be with you in spirit.'

Slowly, Cordelia straightened her grieving limbs and returned to her son's room. John was sitting in a corner, his face grave and pained. Moving next to her boy, she raised his body into her warm arms and kissed his forehead tenderly.

'Thank you my dearest heart for all the joy you have given us. I set you free. Fly to the heavens, into the arms of the blessed Mother.'

The child's eyelids fluttered. He seemed to look at her for a fleeting moment. Suddenly, Cordelia heard an almost imperceptible whooshing sound; soft light poured forth from his delicate face, moving out through the crown of his head. A great peace flooded her soul, dissolving her pain.

'John,' she called softly. 'Come here.'

John too held his child, feeling the peace settle in his heart.

When all the light had left the boy's body, they laid him down with great tenderness. Cordelia ran to tell the old woman, but upon entering the room, she saw the bed was empty. Stepping to the window, she looked up at the sky. Two twinkling lights floated towards heaven, trailing behind them an illuminated thread, which seemed to attach itself right into the centre of her heart. Through her tears, Cordelia smiled, for suddenly she knew that she had been blessed and touched by the hand of God.

The Goddess Cave

There is a place I really love. It is sacred, filled with a silence that teems with strange, subliminal sounds. This place is a cavern, twenty feet under the ground in the centre of the island, where clear water rises and falls to the rhythm of the tides.

Remarkably, the water is not salty, but sweet and fresh, floating like heavenly ambrosia offered by the gods. Sometimes, when I sit there on the cool slab of limestone, I can hear water dripping down the sides of the holy cave, the pointed rocks forming keys like those belonging to a magnificent organ in a sanctified cathedral. The tinkling sounds of tiny rivulets are the bells of priestesses calling me to a life of inner joy. I adore this cave.

In the past, I would take others there hoping to share this feeling of holiness, this magical silence of creation. Initially, it surprised me when they did not honour the stillness or notice the fine frequencies of energy moving through the crystalline air. I realized that sacred space is profoundly personal to every one. It is the eternal zone within that protects us from the stimuli of the temporal world outside. In such a place, we are

self contained and disengaged from the field of time. My cave of bliss is a personal kingdom where I am hermetically sealed off from external voices. I stopped taking just anyone, not out of frustration but merely out of respect for myself.

I become whole when I enter the underground tabernacle where shafts of light illuminate the water with emerald green brilliance. Breathing at my own pace, I travel inward, exploring the mysteries. Strange, but whenever the magic of that cave penetrates my being I feel close to some mystical break-through, some fantastic reflection of where I want to be. It is like touching my invisible centre and, at the same time, my consciousness feels the rapture of expanding into the galaxies.

I have named this place The Goddess Cave. I believe a goddess lives there. Her potion is the elixir of life that urges the spirit to fly. She is a shape-shifter and takes on various forms.

Once, while I was praying, she settled on a rock before me, and taking on the shape of a graceful banana quit, dressed in lemon yellow and green robes, she chirped loudly,

'This is my home. Take care where your feet tread, for one must always respect the hearth of a goddess.'

At other times, she will dart out suddenly, in the form of a black bat, her high-pitched song silencing my erratic thoughts and reprimanding my lack of internal discipline. Yet again, she has appeared before me with soothing arms of light, gracefully dancing upon the walls, embracing me and drawing me deeper into the receptive womb she inhabits. Over and over, she calls me to surrender and die, so that I may be reborn into the light that cascades from above over my mortal body.

Years ago, Lucayan Indians lived in the green woods nearby. Their feet were light upon our golden shores. My bones feel the memory of mythical dances and ritualistic

offerings made to the goddess. I close my eyes and hear singing, chanting. The groaning of copulating men and women explodes in my ears while outside the heat is heavy, hushed and steaming.

In this cave all images are forever holy. I never want to leave, for life is full here even if I do nothing. In the stillness, there is harmony and honesty. All the tensions of daily life dissolve, and in this temple of nature my spirit knows exaltation.

Miriam's Departure

Miriam leaned back with a sigh, her frail fingers absent-mindedly stroking the wine-coloured vinyl of the armchair she was sitting in. Sunlight flickered through the faded hospital curtains, casting a lonely shadow on the bare wall before her. Suddenly, she raised her tired arms to her head to check if her long white braid was in place, but she couldn't remember who had combed her hair.

Where am I?, she wondered for a moment. Slowly, fragments of the morning floated before her eyes. Ah yes, the man in white! He had stood before her and told her something important, something that made her heart jump. She couldn't remember his words, only the feeling. The awful foreboding feeling that made her think of a tiny minnow being chased by a hungry barracuda. The man in white had smiled, but his teeth loomed yellow and nasty. Now, her chest was burning again and an icy tremor was running down her arm.

She bowed her head. Two silent teardrops fell upon the tattered gray blanket that wrapped her knees. Still, she felt cold. Her fingers dabbled in the sparkling drops, drawing the liquid into the shape of a star. She loved the stars! How many nights had she stood by the sapphire sea, looking up at Orion, wondering how the god would feel if she unbuckled his starry belt? She laughed softly now, remembering. But that was so long ago. Her ebony hair, highlighted by the moon, had blown in the wind, looping itself around her mortal lover, tying soft knots around his throat. Scooping Miriam into his lean arms, he carried her to the water's edge, just where the tide formed a natural pool tinged gentian-violet. They lay there, the foam swirling over their naked bodies like hundreds of white belly dancers. She wanted to drink him in, swallow the very soul of him. For in that union, she felt whole and merged with an unknown deity.

A loud knock shattered her reverie.

They always knock when I'm dreaming, but never wait for me to invite them in, she thought dismayed. In this place, everything is so impersonal, so cold. No one has time anymore.

She looked up. The man in white was back. What was he saying? Her heart lurched painfully. He seemed to be chastising her from afar with a voice that was hard and mechanical, nothing like the crooning of the white-crowned pigeons perched in the orange flame tree outside her bedroom window.

'Where am I?' she asked. Her voice sounded like the broken string on a Spanish guitar; no depth or melody, only a sad croak.

'Mrs Roberts,' said the man in white, 'I've asked you several times. Have you no children? Is there no one who can take care of you?'

Miriam gazed up into his eyes. She could see little black

spots in his irises. They made her think of the boll weevils that crawled through her flour when the summer heat was on, and the air in her cupboards stood still. She hated those bugs. They were determined to devour the cornmeal she so carefully sifted. Fumbling for words, she tried to answer, but her tongue would not obey. Only her mind. It spiraled back to the time when she held her baby boy close to her breast. His curls had been so soft, streaked ginger by the sun. Seeing him stretch out his little legs to leap over fallen coconut trunks made her smile with pride. He was the gift brought about by the union with her lover, a union blessed by the angels, until they sent the raging winds that destroyed his boat and sacrificed his spirit to Neptune. His body had been carried deep down into the swirling temple under the sea. Miriam never saw him again, but she remembered his touch on her cheek as sweet as frangipanis bursting forth in winter, and the way his hand cupped the small of her back when they danced calypso in the square. Oh! He knew how to hold her just right; guiding her body to his own rhythm, while giving her the freedom to whirl flamboyantly across the dance floor. Their hips had gyrated under the tropical sky, the Big Dipper bowing low to watch them, while passersby stood still, awed by the spectacle of love.

Again, she felt the pain in her heart, deep purple pain when the sand turned to mud and the sea gulls stopped flying, frozen dead against the turmeric sky. The angels decided to bring her son home, but the waves that transported him ashore were asphalt hard and laden with cruel generosity. She had clasped his slender body in her arms, but his youthful legs no longer straddled her own in playful games. His chubby hands did not pry open her fingers in search of a lemon sweet

she might have hidden there. His eyes, bright as the Chinese lanterns he had begged her to string up in the coconut tree, never smiled at her again.

'Mrs Roberts, you are not taking your digitalis or your painkillers. Look, the tablets are still here on the table. If you don't take your medication, you'll die.'

Miriam looked down at her alabaster hands marked with spots of aging memories. She wriggled her fingers. These were the hands that could twist off a crawfish head without flinching, or filet a yellow fin tuna faster than lightning. Still, they resisted reaching out for the vial containing the small white pills.

'Mrs Roberts,' the nasal voice persisted, 'if you can't give us the name of a family member who can take care of you, you will have to go to an old peoples' home. You are no longer able to look after yourself, and we can't keep you here. You will need to leave tomorrow morning.'

Miriam nodded, bowing her head in resignation. Two more teardrops coursed down her creased cheeks and fell into her upturned palms. The liquid drops made her think of tropical rain, and the joy that filled her when she raced outside her cottage to stand naked under the spouting gutter. Her body had tingled then, and she had scrubbed herself clean with a rough native sponge, running it between her thighs in anticipation of her lover's nightly visits, mango tongue and watermelon kisses. Oh, but she was old now; the skin on her body lax and withered, all the plumpness gone. She felt like a lonely starfish, deserted by the ebbing tide, left behind to shrivel in the waning sun.

The door slammed. She was alone again. Somehow, she felt more comfortable when the man in white left. His company

was scary, and she never liked swimming with sharks, unlike her lover who boldly proclaimed himself a fearless master of the ocean predator world.

'My love,' he would whisper in the obsidian night, 'tomorrow I will dive pearls for you. I will find one the colour of pink flamingos to match the blush in your cheeks.'

'There are sharks where you dive,' she would cry. 'Please, don't put yourself in danger. Your life means more to me than any pearl.'

He had not listened to her plea. Perhaps with her face pressed into the nape of his neck, her voice had become too muffled. The following day he was gone, and her son along with him. The squall that came up out of the northeast was unexpected. It had a mind of its own; vicious, electric, intent on destroying. She remembered standing on the shore and watching the waterspout run down the horizon, like black India ink falling from a boiling cauldron. Her lover and her child were right below that sucking gargoyle. She knew the feeling of helplessness, how it made her belly sink into despair. She had the same feeling now, a sense of descending into blackness.

Evening arrived. Another harsh knock. A nurse came in whistling a tuneless tune.

'Mrs Roberts, your dinner is here.'

A tray was thrust before her. Metal tops removed in a loud clatter. Steam rising, hot from watery vegetable soup.

'Have you got any conch chowder?' Miriam asked politely. 'You know the thick red kind with kernels of corn and the sweet flesh of ground conch?'

It wasn't that Miriam felt hungry, but she would have given anything to smell the pungent spices once more; the

thyme and goat pepper.

The nurse just snorted. 'You'd have to go diving for conch yourself if you want that kind of soup, and you sure don't look like you'd last in the sea for more than a few minutes!'

Once more the door slammed shut. Once more, Miriam was alone, free to dream. Sometime around midnight, she rose. Her joints creaked like the winches on an ancient schooner with billowing sails. She smiled at the sound. Everything was going to be all right. She was going home, despite what the man in white had said. She dressed slowly, but with resolve, pulling her lavender sweater over her head and smoothing down her hair, which still fell in unmanageable strands around her wrinkled cheeks. Searching through her skirt pocket, she found the mother-of-pearl hair clasp that her lover had given her so many years before. Ambling into the bathroom, she switched on the light so that she could wrap the decorative piece around the end of her thick braid. She had kept it hidden because she was afraid some thoughtless person might steal it. It was valuable and she knew it, but she cherished it because it reminded her of his teeth gleaming ivory white in the sun.

I must look my best, she thought, pinching her cheeks for a splash of colour.

I'm going home! Bless the Lord, I'm going home!

Silently, she opened the door and hobbled through the hall and down the stairwell. No one would notice her leaving. Besides, in the morning they would demand that she go. The night felt warm on her dry skin. She loved the humidity. When she was young, it had made her feel sexy and smooth. She remembered licking the tiny pearls of perspiration on her lover's forehead when their dance of passion dissolved.

That was sweetness! Oh yes, that was pure salty sweetness!

As she pushed on through the darkness, Miriam relied entirely on her sense of smell. It would lead her to the sea, of that she was certain.

No matter how old I am, I'll always find the ocean, she thought. The trade winds blowing in from the south call to me, just like a familiar reef calls an old loggerhead turtle home. I'm coming, she whispered silently, I'm coming!

Miriam was breathing hard now, in frequent shallow gasps. She knew the ocean was close. She could smell the salty spray carried on the silky breeze.

Oh, how I have missed the scent of you! she cried. I've missed you so deeply that my heart burns to feel you wrap yourself around me. But I am coming, I promise I am coming!

When her feet touched the powdered sand and thousands of grains filled her shoes, she fell onto her hands and knees and began crawling down the beach slope toward the lapping waves. In the east, dawn was breaking, the sun still withholding its soft, pink rays. Miriam sat back on her withered haunches. Beside her, a sand crab scampered out of its hole, his bright beady eyes regarding her solemnly. She smiled at him, and he seemed to raise his tiny claw in a salute before disappearing back into his underground domain.

Before her eyes, the water stretched over the lagoon in folds of violet chiffon. She remembered the night when she and her lover had taken their marriage vows. Her sarong had been the colour of morning glories, and he had gazed at her deliriously, like a man drunk on passion-fruit wine, unable to keep his hands from roaming over her full breasts.

She giggled into the wind. He had not been able to wait until they reached the cottage, all lit up with candles. No, he had taken her right there in the yard, pushing her into the

rough hammock that swung between two seagrape trees.

'You are my love, my only love,' he had whispered hoarsely. 'We belong together even into the night of eternity.'

Her heart was hurting again, contracting tightly against the wall of her chest.

It's time to go, she thought. It's time!

Slowly she stood. Miriam was old, but her body was still graceful in the morning light, the lines of her face noble and strong. Holding herself erect, like the dancer she had always been, she slid into the amethyst sea. The water smelled menthol cool, and as it rushed over her face, she knew once more the joy of its embrace. Small bubbles floated from her nose as she allowed herself to be drawn into the deep. Suddenly, something moved under her, coming up to meet her withered belly like a black velvet angel.

I should be frightened, Miriam thought, but this feels like heaven.

As she turned her head, Miriam saw the winged tips of a gigantic manta ray.

Oh my Lord, she cried, my chariot has come to take me home!

Her body surrendered, yielding to the creature's graceful movement. Together they skated through the water, Miriam holding fast to the horns that protruded from the manta's head. His skin was soft as cashmere, and he led her just like her lover, swooping in and out of the water, plummeting down and flying up through the air in a climactic splash-dance.

Oh, the ecstasy of it! The freedom, the lightness of spirit.

Further out they travelled, their bodies somersaulting in unison, as they neared the foaming breakers where the ocean kissed the black coral barrier. Finally, the sea ray slowed down. Above her the sky was a painting of oleander blossoms.

She forced her eyes open underwater. Below, lay the broken structure of her lover's boat. She drifted off the gentle monster's back.

'Miguel,' she cried out loud, her voice gurgling into the water, 'I'm here! Miguel, my darling Miguel!'

Rays of light shimmered through the water, illuminating the coral hallways filled with angels. Miriam took one last breath and riding the ocean swell, she fell into the outstretched arms of her lover, eternally grateful to be home, wrapped in his ardent embrace once more. Now that she was with him, she would help him mend the boat. Together they would sail across the sea with pearls streaming behind them. Her eyes fluttered in the jade green liquid.

But wait! Who was that?

Someone was swimming toward her. A young boy with wavy hair, smiling cheeks and dark lashes that curled up toward the emerald surface.

Oh my son, my precious baby! Come here to Mama. Never again will I let you go. You're home! Daddy's home! I'm home too! Praise God!

And the bubbles that escaped her lips floated up to greet the day in a silent song of gratitude.

Sunset

Mockingbirds serenading the day before darkness falls. Flashes of purple opening into a deep azure sky. Portals to another world.

On my balcony, I bask in the golden rays fading into heaven's dome. Inside, behind glass doors, my son plucks the strings of an old classical guitar. Measures of *Silent Night* float into the humid air; accompaniment for the feathered recital.

The first bombs struck Kabul, Afghanistan, this evening. Silver gray machines flying at breakneck speed. I can almost hear the whining, popping sounds, exploding into the Middle Eastern night. Nothing silent about that.

Here the evening is peacefully laden with benevolence. Splashes of pink and orange fan the water below, running across the mirrored surface like Gauguin's oils. Oh! What's that sound? A splash disturbs my reverie. Splosh! Plop! What creature might that be, vying for my attention? A blue runner? A moray eel? A barracuda?

I lean over my balustrade, the metal hard against my belly. Two magnificent eagle rays are gracefully dancing past on

silent, spotted wings. I want to laugh with elation as they glide into the ocean's ballroom.

Oh my primal friends! You have been here since the beginning, moving through time, never losing yourself to mankind's destructive dance. How do you do this? Teach us! We have so much to learn from you. You make no attempt to control each other, yet you waltz in perfect unison, all the while remaining free.

Above me, a night swallow dives with swift precision, catching mosquitoes for dinner. Sweet-feathered friend, you kill for survival, never in the name of God or for some Holy War. The concept 'God' doesn't even exist in you. You simply soar without knowing.

Over yonder stands my favourite, solitary seagrape tree. For some odd reason, it grows out of the sand like an oversized Japanese bonsai, dressed in a green silk kimono. So foreign, yet so much a part of my world. You remind me that, although we stand alone, we are all One.

Giant palm fronds, nudged by the salty breeze, fan my head, swooping across the violet sky like mighty steeds. Clouds, like costumed actors, float over the illuminated stage. An armadillo pushing a feathery ball with its long snout, followed by a sleeping camel, create the scene. What fun to let the imagination wander! Why don't I do this more often?

The tranquility restores my soul. I am beside the still water, resting in the valley of Eden.

The earth spinning from sunset to sunset. Each one unique. Imagine this—a mind-boggling thought—never has one sunset been the same as another. Myriad of colours, ever-changing, pouring forth from one source. Are we not the same, we humans? Indeed, we are born dressed in the various shades of man, speaking different languages and believing in

diverse philosophies and yet, the human heart, the essence of humanity, is ever nourished by one eternal fountain. If we could accept, simply accept without striving to change the others, then we could see that every difference is a unique colour added to the canvas of life's sunset.

'Dem Island Tings'

Simple Sesame Salad

Important: If you live in The Bahamas, the ingredients required for this salad might require a prayer for divine manifestation!

Ingredients
Romaine lettuce
Spinach leaves
Arugula
Shredded carrots (*just for colour*)
Crumbled Gorgonzola (*Well actually, flexibility
    is the key. Feta or Bleu Cheese will do.*)
Handful of walnuts (*On second thought, almonds
    or cashews will do.*)
Crisp Fuji apple cut into thin strips (*Don't worry!
    Granny Smith, Gala, whatever!*)

Dressing
1/4 cup olive oil
1/4 cup seasoned sushi rice vinegar
Generous dash of toasted sesame oil
Dash of 100% pure maple syrup
    (*not Aunt Jemima's smiling face kind*)
Dash of whipping cream
Teaspoon of Dijon mustard
Lawries garlic salt
Pepper

If you still have the strength, after spending your day shopping at our various markets, then shake the dressing in a jar and pour lovingly over your greens. Enjoy!

Bahamian Salad Saga

Anyone living in The Bahamas knows the stress created by the task of making a simple salad. It should be such an easy thing, right? Run to the supermarket, buy the necessary ingredients, come home to your cool kitchen and proceed with your recipe. But let me tell you, the invisible culinary divas have something else in store for you! Making a simple salad becomes a sisyphean task, requiring physical stamina, inexhaustible patience, a healthy wallet and a full tank of gas!

You might think that, by now, I would have learned the lesson that, in paradise, planned dishes are a virtual impossibility, but it isn't so. Every week I am still feverishly hopeful; a hope stemming from my insatiable desire for healthy greens.

My step appears light and jaunty on Fridays, as I run down the stairs to my car.

'Today will be a good day,' I say to myself, preparing to manifest the fulfillment of my week-long cravings.

The trailers have arrived, filled with fresh produce from America. Tonight, I'll chew on crunchy leaves and delectable walnuts, savouring Gorgonzola as it melts in my mouth.

But a silent, emphatic voice niggles in my ear,
'Dream on, sister,' and I try not to listen.

My first stop is Solomon Brothers. The extreme heat forces me to begin shopping at the store furthest from home, so that I may, at least, be headed in the direction of my refrigerator when I exit those doors and continue my rounds. In The Bahamas, you have to move quickly once you have perishables in the trunk.

'Good morning,' I say to the security officer, who sits comfortably on a stool outside this huge warehouse. His name is Cordial and really, of all the security officers I see there, he is by far the most cordial. Our brief conversations always begin with a laugh, and a plunge into the political topic of the day.

'Seems like de fresh wind de government promised us done stop blowin!' he says grinning. 'Only breeze I feel now is de one comin' from de South!'

We both chuckle loudly and then, trying to maintain my sense of humour, I brace myself in anticipation of the smell that will assault my nose when I walk through those doors.

Inside, I take small sniffs of air, hoping not to gag. I want to shout,

'Why the devil must a food store be so smelly?'

The little voice says, 'Don't go there, sister! Your question is not part of the solution!'

Okay, and off I head towards the fresh produce. Fresh produce! Sounds great, doesn't it? Well, if I am very lucky, the produce will be less than a week old. Usually though, the Romaine lettuce I am so eagerly seeking will carry a sticker that says 50% off. In America, this would be a sweet deal, but my heart sinks because at Solomons, this price indicates that the package has been there for three weeks or more. I cringe to

recall that in my great need, I have, on odd occasion, actually turned the bag over and over in my hands, as though with this gesture I might banish the wilt; and then, because of my over-whelming addiction to anything green, I have placed that same bag into the large, blue shopping cart before me. Inevitably, the cart I have chosen has bent wheels, and as I push forward, I find myself straining all the muscles of one arm to avoid sliding away in the opposite direction of where I want to go.

Now, Solomons also has a 'Salad Fresh' cooler that stands in the far aisle against the wall. Sometimes, just sometimes, it is filled with small bags of pre-washed salad containing a divine mixture of romaine lettuce, arugula, spinach leaves and shredded carrots. These precious bags are actually what prompted the creation of my simple salad. I only needed to tear open a bag and behold! No rinsing, slicing or scrutinizing! I am not sure what inspired the buyers to import these horticultural delicacies, but on the day I saw them, I fell into salad rapture! Shoppers nearby were showered with a variety of excited 'oohs' and 'wows!' The fact that I paid $4.99 for one small bag did not stop me from buying six bags at once. Money is of no conse-quence when you have an addiction, and the satisfaction of my palate warrants almost any cost. Filled with zest and hope, I ran into the manager's office, waving the 'Tender Trio' package and begged him to continue ordering this item.

'Okay Ma'am. I promise we'll do that.'

Elated, I hurried back the following week, but all hope wilted when I saw the bare shelves displaying one or two packages of greens, now reduced to decaying slime. The sight left me irritable for days, evidence of my green depression. But let me carry on.

Supposing, just supposing fortune has smiled on me, and I

exit Solomons with edible salad, then my next stop will be Butler Specialty Foods. Unless, of course, I need wine, in which case I drive across the street to Bristol Cellars. Pulling out the salad from the bags of groceries, I place it directly in line with my air conditioning vent. While the car is running, I race into the shop to purchase a bottle. If my favourite bottle of Merlot is there, I consider myself lucky, but should it be sold out, then disaster strikes and I stand bewildered before the rows of red wine, never knowing which one to choose. Meanwhile, my imaginary eye is psychically checking on the salad struggling to stay alive in the car. Finally my saviour, Jimmy, the icon behind the cash register, sees how perplexed I am and calls out,

'What are you looking for today?'

'A good Merlot,' I say, trying to contain myself before I snap, 'where the hell is the one I always buy?'

Hastily grabbing the bottle he suggests, I pay and rush out to check on the precious salad bag, as though it were a distressed infant. Later, my husband, who has no concept of the anxiety food shopping elicits in my psyche, will ask me why I'm so wiped out.

Continuing on, I make my way to Yellow Pine Street, managing to turn right into Butler's parking lot, just before the cars hurtling around that sharp curve send me flying to my death. I would hate to see my greens squashed on the steaming pavement after coming this far.

Butlers is a fine store, and those of us who live on Grand Bahama are grateful for the variety of food wares stocked in that tiny space. The fact that the aisles are so narrow you have to be anorexic to pass through them is of no great concern to anyone.

Placing my basket at the end of the aisle, I fill my arms with

curries, mango chutney, Dijon mustard, miso paste, bags of organic brown rice and walnuts, which, though used sparingly, are a must for my salad but can only be purchased in 3 lb. bags. Staggering back, I squeeze past fellow shoppers. Usually, I find myself face to face with a friend and in passing, we give each other a quick peck on the cheek. Shopping this way takes care of social obligations. Of course, this contact is far less pleasant if you feel like you're having a bad hair day, or the person whose face is only inches away from yours is someone you've been trying to avoid for some time.

Toasted sesame oil is an essential ingredient for my simple salad. Without this nutty, exotic flavour, the salad dressing falls miserably flat, yet this item seems to vanish off the shelves faster than the speed of light. I often wonder why, because no one I know even uses sesame oil. Once I discover that not one bottle remains on the designated shelf, my search for the elusive oil begins. I become a detective, sniffing around every can, lifting objects, praying for a clue. Sometimes, I am given a reprieve, and one dusty bottle will be hiding somewhere way in the back of a shelf. Usually, I am forced to search out the manager in the office and urge her to order this necessity. I have waited eight weeks for toasted sesame oil. Eight weeks! That's two months! This phenomenon has led me to buy ten bottles at a time; a purchase, which not only adds sixty dollars to my grocery bill, but creates havoc in my small pantry. But at least I have it!

The same process holds true for sushi vinegar, but because it's easier to find, I stock only five bottles. I'm ashamed to say, that my devious lower self has been known to conceal a few bottles around the store so that no one else can find them. Why, you ask, does the recipe call for Japanese vinegar? Well, it's less acidic than balsamic vinegar, and after this shopping

spree, I'm prone to heartburn.

Okay, now I need 100% pure maple syrup. Aunt Jemima just doesn't do the trick. In spite of her natural smile, the syrup tastes artificial. I round the tight corner. Hallelujah! It's there! But my joy soon wanes when all I spy are half gallon jugs, and I imagine myself later in the day, kneeling on hard tiles, painstakingly reorganizing my crowded refrigerator to make space.

'Never mind,' says the commanding voice in my head. 'Just take it!' Another $18.99 added to my bill!

My basket overflowing, I step in line behind a gentleman who obviously has the hots for Bernadette, the pretty cashier. As he flirts with her, she giggles, but I am in no mood for this romantic interlude. My greens are suffering outside. I clear my throat, look at my watch, and Bernadette gets the message. I pay, not even blinking at the grand total. That's what chequebooks are for! If you were to study my cheque register, you would see that every cent I earn is spent at four vendors only: Solomons, Bristol Cellars, Butlers and Winn Dixie—the latter of which is next on my agenda.

Solomon's lingering odour accompanies me as I drive all the way uptown. As I pull into the Winn Dixie plaza, my eyes dart around desperately searching for a pushcart. It seems that whenever I enter that store, all the carts have mysteriously disappeared. Employees will stand chatting and laughing right where the carts ought to be stationed, but no one sees the importance of this shopping aid. I have long since given up asking for a cart, because the man in charge will look at me as though I'm crazy, and point to a broken one leaning haphazardly on the curb, at the far end of the car park.

Once inside, I zoom over to the fruits. What I need now are crisp Fuji apples, which will be sliced into thin strips and used to garnish my salad. I imagine biting into one, feeling the juice dribble down my chin. Big negative! The Fuji apples look like miniature, wizened heads. More often than not, if they're not shrunken, they'll be badly bruised, emblazoned with scars made by someone's fingernails. Of course, all I can think of is the bacteria festering in these cuts. I rummage around until I find one or two that pass the grade. The grade! That reminds me, why must we Bahamian consumers be subjected to second grade fruits and vegetables?

'Oh there you go again!' says the impatient voice. 'Stop whining. Your life's not so bad. Do you have apples? Do you have salad? Do you have specialty items like toasted sesame oil?'

I nod.

'Then be quiet!'

Okay, I zip over to the dairy products. En route, I pick up a one pound jar of Lawries garlic salt because—you guessed it—they're out of the smaller sizes. No problem!

Now to the whipping cream. McArthur's ultra-pasteurized is generally in stock, even in half-pint sizes. What a blessing! The only catch to this product is that you're dead if you don't check the date! I can't count the many times I arrived home eager to make my dressing, and opened the little flap only to find a congealed mass of disgusting, white curds. A small occurrence that only enhances my sour mood.

Racing to the cash register, I place my items on the belt, instinctively choosing the one that does not roll. My cashier lady slouches on her stool, calling over to her colleague that she will be having pigs feet souse for dinner tonight. All I want is a salad sweetie! Sipping coke from a cool can, she lazily gestures for me to push the items toward her, while I struggle inwardly, trying not to run hot under the collar.

But wait! At the sight of her fingernails, I am suddenly fascinated. Entire works of art are painted on these three-inch long acrylic extensions. So what if the cash register keys can't be pressed down! I keep quiet. Those claws are formidable. A spontaneous question crosses my mind. How on earth does she wipe her backside with those nails? Oh no, don't go there! I think about the nail marks in my apples. More festering bacteria! The five mini paintings move, handing me food stamps, and I'm jolted back into reality. My box at home is crammed full of these bonus stamps, accumulated over the years, yet I continue to hoard them, deluding myself that one day I will have time to lick and stick the many hundreds onto paper sheets. Why the hell doesn't the supermarket just lower the prices instead of torturing me with nonsensical labour?

'Oh for God's sakes woman, stop griping!' snarls my annoyed critic.

I leave Winn Dixie, relieved to have completed my mission. Home sweet home! My last task will be to haul ten bags of groceries up the stairs. I try to think of it as a workout, my own keep fit program! Humming a merry tune, I unpack everything. The greens look a bit like soggy socks, but they'll do. Suddenly, I stop dead in my tracks between the sink and the granite counter! Oh no! I forgot the cheese. I can't eat the salad without crumbled Gorgonzola. It's not the same! What would Martha Stewart do? Frantically, I search the cheese box and find an old piece of veined Danish Blue. It's either the Danish Blue crumbling, or me falling apart. I choose the cheese.

Evening falls. Outside on my verandah, rose sunlight settles over my dinner table like gossamer cloth. The ocean before me flows in streaks of red wine, while I sit quietly gazing at the

bounteous gifts nature provides. Green palm fronds fan my face as I dwell in God's fruitful garden. Coconuts hang like huge globes waiting to be picked, their sweet milk contained in green chalices. Embraced by such fullness, I swear I will never complain again. Remnants of exasperation melt with the setting sun, and I recall what is truly important. At the end of the day, do I not have it all? Do I not have everything I need to celebrate life? I lack nothing. Supper awaits me.

Before saying grace, I take my husband's hand and sneak a peak at the greens nestled in my wooden bowl, thankful for God's colourful kitchen of life, for the way it prepares me while teaching me patience seasoned with humour.

Cockroach Conniption

Truly, there is nothing that upsets my stomach more than a big, fat cockroach crawling across the floor. Nothing turns my flesh into acres of goose bumps more than a brown cockroach climbing the wall, displaying his hairy legs. I cannot say that I am merely frightened. No! The fear I feel when I see one of these repugnant creations of nature is more akin to absolute terror; a terror so intense that I am paralyzed. The paralysis that overcomes my limbs is even more deadly because I am unable to kill the beast. So there I am in a room, it might be any room, and I am rendered utterly powerless against the invading insect. That such a small creature holds this huge capacity to unnerve me, is a riddle.

But I know the exact instant when this intimidation started. I still shudder at the memory. I was a little girl, eight years old at most. It was a warm summer night, the sweet smell of Bahamian jasmine wafted through my window, drugging my senses. I slept the way children do after a day of playing in the waves, limbs askew, hair flung out on white pillows, mouth open, breathing into the world of dreams. A little river of

saliva trickled from my lips. The muscles of my face were slack, as something began to tickle me into wakefulness.

At first I thought I was only dreaming, but soon, I heard a small, squeaking noise. My eyes fluttered open. Something was sucking at the vermillion border of my lips! My hand flew to my face, but the creature was tenacious, biting into my pink flesh. I screamed, my little fingers plucking wildly at the object. Nothing could have prepared me for that moment, in which my childish perceptions were changed forever. Terrified, I leaped out of bed, and in the moonlight, I saw the hideous form of an enormous cockroach fly from my face onto the sheets and disappear behind the headboard. The idea of that grotesque animal gorging himself on my saliva, as though it were a Slurpy, made my blood freeze. I was a changed girl. Shrieking at the top of my lungs, I raced to the bathroom and hid under the sink between the soft towels. My father, who thought a burglar had entered the house, suddenly appeared, brandishing a shotgun!

'Kill him Papi,' I screamed, as he pulled open the door to my hiding place. 'Please, kill him!'

'Who was it?' he cried.

'A cockroach! A big cockroach!'

I don't remember whether my father killed the culprit or not, but surely that moment marked the beginning of my life-long cockroach phobia. I was never to be the same trusting child. I began to question God's intelligence. Why would He create such repulsive things to plague those who peacefully inhabited His kingdom? And, of course, I did not recognize the hidden power in the old saying,

'That which you fear most, will always find you.'

From that dark night onward, cockroaches seemed to seek

me out, literally persecute me with collective glee. Paranoid of being attacked by such a bug, I was never again able to enter a dark room. If, perchance, a light bulb blew when I flicked the switch, I became a babbling idiot, pleading for help.

In later years, I lived in New York City where cockroaches seem to be accepted citizens. One morning, as I was meditating in my upper west-side apartment, I glanced at the floor. Bad move when you're doing spiritual practice! There, staring me in the eye, challenging my tranquility, was a brazen roach, boldly twitching his feelers. Any possible flow of mystical energy trying to make its way up my spine froze, chilling every nerve. I screamed. He, on the other hand, scuttled merrily across the oak floor, into the bathroom.

'Kill it,' I yelled.

'Kill what?' came my husband's muffled reply from behind the bathroom door.

'A roach! A monster roach! He just crawled under your door!'

'Oh! Okay!'

I heard the muted shuffling of feet, followed by a slipper slapping the floor and the toilet flushing. But you see, when I'm afraid, my extra-sensory perception is heightened. I knew that the man I married had not killed that roach.

'He's dead!' he cried.

'You're lying!' I exclaimed.

'Come on, sweetie, I wouldn't do that to you. I know how roaches scare you.'

But my hair was standing on end and my flesh was crawling all over me. Gingerly, I crossed the room. Suddenly, the same antagonist ran over my foot with lightening speed, and another death cry escaped me. Ripping open the bathroom door, I roared at my husband.

'If ever again you pretend to kill a roach, I'll divorce you on grounds of deception! If you want to stay married to me, you better be man enough to kill the beast!'

'Well, if you hate them so much, why don't you kill them yourself?' he fired back.

'I can't!' I wailed, collapsing on the toilet. 'I'm just too scared to kill them! Give me a snake, a spider, a scorpion, anything but a roach!'

'But sweetheart, that wasn't even a roach, it was a palmetto bug.'

Oh my God! Has anyone ever noticed that when people don't want to talk about cockroaches, they call them palmetto bugs? As if that form of identification makes the unsightly creature more acceptable.

'Oh no,' they'll remark in a condescending tone, 'we don't have cockroaches here, only palmetto bugs. They are a different insect altogether because they can fly.'

Well, as far as I'm concerned, a cockroach is a cockroach, and one that flies is just that much more disgusting. So, don't try to make them sound exotic!

It is an awful thing to be so helpless in the face of something so small. When I see a cockroach, I am crippled. I would rather face a row of rifles than one single cockroach. Nothing terrifies me more than finding a roach in my bedroom. Immediately, upon spying one, I freeze, because I am certain that this beast has come to terrorize only me. He has come to transport my soul to cockroach hell, and so he is the ultimate enemy. My mind becomes a jellyfish and my courage dwindles. The roach will usually scramble forward a few inches to make sure I am positively focused on him. I know that he is watching me closely, assessing my every move. I may be bigger

than he is, but he knows that in this war, he will be the victorious general. Bobbing his armoured body up and down like a mini army tank, he turns me into a spineless prisoner.

Disgusted at my own lack of leadership, I notice my unsure hand attempting to grasp an object, while my eyes remain locked on the enemy in sick fascination. Feet rooted to the floor, I contort my body to try and grab a shoe or a book. Then, like some palsied warrior, I throw my weapon; an action which to this day has never once managed to kill my foe. On the contrary, now the cockroach's wings are ruffled, and he becomes a stealth-bomber, forcing me to cower in the corner like some blubbering fool. At that point, my only recourse is to run out of the room, slam the door and begin hunting for a weapon of mass destruction. Armed with a can of deadly Raid, I enter the room once more, feeling like Hitler or Saddam Hussein, mean and white-livered. Systematically, I begin to spray the nerve gas, not caring whether the battle I'm fighting is a cowardly one.

In a short while, the cockroach appears, running amok in circles on the floor, trying desperately to shake the oily poison off his wings. I watch, mesmerized by his death dance, but unable to put him out of his misery. I just can't do it! For me, this is an impossible feat. Indeed, I can somersault out of a plane twelve thousand feet above the ground, but I simply cannot move my foot toward that detestable creature to stomp on it. I can't bear to hear the final crunch!

Even after the roach is stone dead, I don't have it in me to pick him up with a tissue and flush him down the toilet. In my mind's eye, I see him crawling back out of the bowl to settle on my backside the next time that I am having a tinkle. That vengeful maneuver, strategically performed by the roach, would certainly be the death of me!

Rainstorm

Seagulls hover above, cawing at the warm air, while just below me in the green water, sea fans sway back and forth, dancing in the sultry currents. There is a peacefulness in the air, no storm forecast. In the background, I hear the song, *A Whiter Shade of Pale* by Procol Harem. The music transports me back in time, into my teenage world; close dancing, heavy breathing, and the ever present longing to be as pretty as my girlfriends, to be the one held in a warm embrace even if my face was uncomfortably pressed against a sweaty cheek.

I was always the one on the outside looking in. Huddled back against the wall, freckle faced, chubby, and so insecure that even now the embarrassment of that time ties my tongue in knots. My mother tried to tell me that a face without freckles was like a sky without stars, but I knew she was trying to comfort me and ease the unbearable shame. I can still feel the tightness welling up through my body, the extreme lack of confidence, coupled with the need to be seen and desired like other girls. They were so ready, so well informed. Applying their wit and sensuality like lip-gloss, they were able to meet

any challenge and play the game of enticement.

As I lean against the soft boat cushions, old pictures run movies in my mind. I feel a subtle shift in temperature. The breeze suddenly cools, becoming more pronounced against my skin. The salty smell of sea gives way to the fresh scent of oncoming rain. I open my eyes. To the north, a black cloud rears up, obscuring the sun, stretching itself out like a mighty Poseidon temple, commanding the sun to go inside, while to the south, the wind begins whipping across the water's surface forming plumed chariots of spray.

In an instant, my reverie is transformed into a world of action. The boat's anchor begins to drag, and with the rising wind, we are drifting dangerously close to the rocky shore. Muscles tense, engines rev, and the anchor is quickly hoisted so that we can move back out to deeper water.

Loud claps of thunder resound in my ears and bright streaks of fluorescent lightning cascade everywhere, like blood vessels bursting under pressure. Tension all around. The sky is being torn asunder by searing flashes of light. Desperately, we attempt to lash down the flapping plastic windows to create a safe hiding place away from the stinging needles of rain, which burn our faces and hands.

The rain is so heavy; visibility becomes an impenetrable gray blanket shrouded in mist. I pray silently that we will be safe. Here in the islands, gale force winds arise without warning, howling like hungry wolves. Treacherous rain spouts suck up any objects in their way and spew them out, after grinding everything to a pulp. Torrential downpours set upon us so quickly that even our thoughts are drowned. No time for anything except action!

A bottle of Jacob's Creek Merlot rolls back and forth,

clanking loudly in the stern. I bend to pick it up, before it breaks and bleeds all over the hull. I feel the chill in my bones, but the towels are soaked. Water streams in through the seams where zippers fight to hold the boat covering together.

I strain my eyes, peering through the smeared plastic windows. I can't even see my hand before my face. Do I hear an engine? Is there another boat close by? Yes ... I think so. We must be careful not to collide.

The ocean is stirred up now. Angry white waves roll like artillery tanks over the bow. Pitching, falling. A bolt of fear runs through me.

Will we capsize?

I have weathered these storms so many times in my life, but each one brings with it a moment of uncertainty, the inner gasp at nature's power—the strength and relentlessness of the wind and sea. There is something awe-inspiring about nature, for it has no favourites—it does not matter whether you are kind or cruel. When the sea rises, it takes us all by surprise. The tides have no personal preference when they pull you beneath the surface. You are not even at their mercy, for they care naught for your soul. No heart can withstand the tempest when it chooses to blow the body into oblivion.

It is this mighty detachment of the elements that makes me feel so small, so invisible, so willing to bow with respect. I am a sea oat stalk flattened by the wind, or a piece of driftwood rising and falling in the heaving waves. I bow before nature's countenance. I surrender my will and pray—please spare me. Standing naked before the elements, I recognize my frailty, yet I am empowered by the feeling of humility.

Gradually, the wind slackens. The man-made sound of a

mobile phone vibrates through the air. Someone is calling to ask if we are safe.

I crawl out through the narrow gate to the backboard. The rain is softer now. I dangle my feet into the sea. It feels like a warm bathtub. Memories of my childhood pour through me. There is something about this kind of experience that always remains with us. It is imprinted in our bones, in the nuclei of our cells, and in the fascia of our lives. The body always remembers. Even if I were to lose my sight, my hearing, and my ability to move, my body would forever contain the experience of a Bahamian storm. This invisible knowledge is omnipresent— it is a part of me, part of my past and my future.

I quiver with cold. Sliding down, I drop beneath the surface, the velvety warmth of the sea wraps my skin. It amazes me that the water feels so warm, when outside the air is chilling. My face pushes up toward the sky, salty rivers flowing out of my mouth. I open my eyes to see tiny figures forming, as droplets of rain plop into the ocean. They look like dancers flitting across the dance floor. As a child, I watched these figures for as long as the rain lasted.

Oh, to be a child again! To watch these things, giving them time to create patterns in the self. To feel the presence of God in the raindrops without wondering if God is there. That is how the rain has touched me. On some deep level, it has given me a sense of Self, washing away the childish fear of never being enough. It has filled me, and when I am emptied by forgetfulness, the rain washes me back into the vast ocean of consciousness from which I have come, reminding me that I am one with everything that moves, even that which quivers silently in the unseen depths.

The Aftermath

Blessed am I, gone the wind's wrath,
Yet I stand crippled in the aftermath.
My body raw, compressed by the storm,
My joints on fire, I want to go home,
Home, to the place where peace abides
And celestial wings stem the tides that surge in me.

The smells of decay, the mold on the walls,
The ceilings still hanging by threads in the halls,
The towels once used to dry myself clean,
Hang soggy and filthy from exposed wooden beams.
Yet blessed am I, for the winds of wrath
Have left me alive in the aftermath.

I look out to sea where once the soft waves,
Played soothing melodies on invisible staves.
An opera emerges discordant and fierce,
Bashing my eardrums with staccatos that pierce.
But blessed am I for the waves come and go
And I am still breathing in the after flow.

Sand In My Shoes

A war zone surrounds me, trees are burnt bare,
Holes gape in houses, it doesn't seem fair,
Not one storm but two have blown us apart!
Displaced are the faces, wind-burned the hearts.
My bones feel the weight of the storm on its path,
Cleaning up fragments in the aftermath.

The day is spent simply in trying to live,
What can I take, what can I give?
Everywhere people seem tired and worn,
Fatigue and exhaustion have become the norm.
Depressed, I fall through a stagnant black hole,
Lost in the aftermath, out of control.

But hark! There's a mockingbird whistling her tune,
Above me last night stood the pregnant full moon.
The east parts the curtain and night greets the day
While the promise of dawn invites me to stay, present,
With feelings of hope and despair,
Steeped in the aftermath after the scare.

Form as I knew it is now empty space,
The old swept away without leaving a trace.
I stand on the sand that shifts with the tide
Knowing I may not concretize
Any belief or structure I hold,
For God in His greatness can always remold
My life, and all that it means.

Yellow Crowned Night Heron

Solitary figure. Night sentinel greeting the dawn, ensuring the diurnal rise of the sun. What called me from my dreams this morning? Stumbling, eyes still heavy with sleep, I rolled out of the shadows, feet searching for sandals, the urge so strong that not even the tantalizing smell of coffee could restrain me. Stepping outside, I felt the balmy air caress my face and moisten my eyes with a few tender raindrops. Welcome dew that cools and smoothes away my wrinkles. Drawn to the beach, I was momentarily anxious that I might miss the sunrise, so I quickened my pace.

There he stood, perfectly still, head bowed in prayer as the sky filled itself with colour. I did not surprise him—he surprised me. Motionless, a living statue. Did he know that I too had come to salute the essence of God? I stopped. Watching, waiting, I saw him take notice of me, black eyes flashing, blinking fiercely.

'When you enter God's territory, do it slowly and in silence, for such is the movement of the soul,' he seemed to command.

Ah! Slender being, fragment of God's myriad creations. You remind me to follow my soul and acknowledge the truth of every moment. How quick I am to let my body rush along on the heels of an impetuous mind.

We stared at each other for what seemed an eternal moment. He held me at bay, proud, unattached, distinguished in his solitude, finally taking one stalking step to the side, allowing me to pass into the holy realm. I bowed my head respectfully, grateful that he deemed me worthy of moving beyond his invisible boundary.

On the beach, cool sand touched my feet, grains packed hard by the night rain. Waves stretched to caress my toes, uncoiling like undulating serpents, softly hissing their song into the air. Above me, giant cotton powder puffs exploded into rose coloured threads, wrapping themselves around curtains of peach silk.

The stillness of it! The simultaneous organza of beauty, the great gift so generously bestowed each day without fail. Terraces of gilded saffron leading into the heavens, beckoning me to rise and journey forward, eyes filling with gratitude.

After some time, I rose, prepared to seize the day. Retracing my footprints, I returned to see the yellow crowned night heron waiting for me. I was hurried now, appointments to be met. I wanted to steal past him, but he had no tolerance for my impatience.

Ruffling his feathers, he threw me a disdainful look and, turning away, flew up towards the new sun, leaving me with a sense of my human inability to simply be, and enjoy the magic for a moment longer.

Tides of Life

Sand In My Shoes

Deliberate Conception

I have always loved elegance and comfort, and so before entering this earthly realm, my determined soul decided that the Hotel Fontainebleau in Miami would be the perfect place for my conception. It must have been in the heat of August 1953, because nine months later, I was gently lifted from my mother's womb, by way of Caesarian section, without having to push my way into this world.

My mother really wanted me. Her longing for a baby girl was so intense that, in spite of being told she must never have babies again, she proceeded to lure my father away from their primitive island life to champagne, caviar and glittering chandeliers at the Hotel Fontainebleau.

Even the sound of the word Fon ... taine ... bleu sounds sexy, don't you think? Sort of a roll and a slur, with a sassy kick at the end. In my mind, I imagine Marilyn Monroe look-a-likes, lips pouting invitations, while hips sway seductively to the rich notes of samba-rendering saxophones played by virile, Latin demigods. Perhaps this explains my lifelong penchant for dark haired men! But let's return to the story.

There I was, having just flown in from eternity, floating

above the dance floor, a mere ball of energy already thinking,

'Ooh, when I get there, I want a man that looks like the one kissing that instrument!'

I have never imagined my mother to be scintillatingly sexy. In a totally inappropriate moment, my father told me that once, while he was being amorous with her, she suddenly stopped, and looking him straight in the eye, cried out,

'Oh my God! I forgot to close the chicken coop!'

Perish the picture! Who of us can honestly imagine our parents doing it? It's too close to home, and so irreverent!

But done it, they did! I am living proof!

When I look back on some of the things my parents told me regarding their personal experiences, I am both uncomfortable and amused. I often wonder how suitable it is for little ears to hear intimate details of their parents' lives. Parents are, after all, the authority, the ambient field of God that holds us while we are young, and knowing too much has a way of making us cringe.

However, be that as it may, my mother was determined to have another child, and in her heart of hearts, she trusted that this new baby would be a girl. Two rough and tumble boys filled her home with cowboy games, loud drumming, explosive rages, and squeals of laughter, yet her desire for a girl never faltered. The opinions of several medical doctors who told her she might die if she went through another pregnancy were tossed into the wind like confetti.

My father, also a doctor, was very concerned, and never once did he forget to take precautions, lest one busy sperm, intent on fertilization, made its way up into the receptive cave.

But as the Bahamian people say, 'woman smarter den de man,' and so my mother began to think of a way to outsmart the masculine, medical world. Carefully calculating the moment of ovum release, she planned a trip to Miami, feigning a desperate

need to buy new clothes for her boys, as well as supplies to make life on the island more bearable.

'You could use a break,' she said generously to my father. 'You are seeing far too many patients, and you look exhausted. Let's leave the boys with the housekeeper and go!'

Meanwhile, she saved every penny possible, quietly sneaking one pound notes out of the white envelope he used to store his money. He always pretended not to know.

With her most revealing lingerie packed safely in her suitcase, she and my father drove to the airport. The airport on the island consisted of a single runway, shabbily paved, and one tiny shack, which served as a terminal for all international flights. Together they boarded a rickety DC 10 operated by Mackey Airlines, and off they flew to the big city. I imagine that after living in thick, humid heat amongst mosquitoes and sand-flies, the air conditioning in the hotel must have felt like blue heaven. In the evening, seated in the lap of dining room luxury, they were served oysters with chilled Mouton Cadet; a delicious aphrodisiac fit for the gods.

My mother ordered his favourite Canadian Club whisky, more wine, and even sweet liqueur. Making sure his glass was never empty, she raised her own and toasted life. When he was quite tipsy, she led him to the dance floor, filling his head with romantic memories of the days when they first met. How far they had come from war-torn Germany to the Hotel Fontainebleau! It does not take much for a woman to seduce a man, even when that woman is my own mother. I simply cannot imagine what techniques she used to light his fire. You can conjure those pictures yourselves!

Suffice it to say, that after ample quantities of whisky, wine and Crème de Menthe, she literally dragged him up to the room, probably by the seat of his pants, which she soon proceeded to

remove. Easing him onto the flowered bedspread, she smiled, thinking of the plan she had devised. Opening her pocketbook, she found the pack of condoms she had secretly purchased that afternoon and laughing, she waved one in front of his glazed eyes.

Please don't ask me what kind of condoms they were. I guess Durex was the primary producer of these safety balloons even then, but I have no idea if they smelled of mint or strawberries, or if the rubber contained pleasure-enhancing bumps! My mind simply cannot wrap itself around those details. What I do know is that, in spite of his drunken state, she wanted him to think that safety still mattered.

'Prevention is worth an ounce of cure,' she giggled.

Of course, he was oblivious to the fact that when she disappeared into the bathroom to slip on her next-to-nothing nightie, she also whipped a sewing kit out of her cosmetic case and prying it open, removed a sharp needle. Jabbing holes into the end of that protective lining, my mother created a doorway for my life. She returned with a come-hither glow, and securing the hose in its proper position, she lay back on the luxurious pillows, leaving everything else to Fate. The waters of life were allowed to flow through that tiny portal and my soul, hungry as it was, seized the opportunity to begin its sojourn here on earth.

Three months later, when my sweet little fetus was swimming safely in her womb, my mother told my father that she was pregnant.

'How could this happen?' he asked, concerned.

'Well,' she replied, 'I believe it takes two to tango! I'm sure you know how it happened.' Then, averting her gaze coyly, she added, 'But with these man-made precautions, you can never be one hundred percent sure!'

By this time, I was more than just the twinkle in her eye.

Sand In My Shoes

When Death Comes Smiling

Growing up in The Bahamas as the daughter of Abaco's island doctor, I came to see death as an intrinsic part of life. It was a subject that was discussed both respectfully and fearlessly in our home. In such a small place, where everyone was acquainted, we all knew whose family had been touched by death's cold hand. I became acutely aware of my father's feelings when he cared for a dying patient. These were people he had looked after for years. These were the children he had delivered into the world; the mothers who laughed and cried when they first saw their newborn babies; the fathers who worked hard fishing, farming or building businesses to support those they loved. He hated to see anyone suffer; although his patience ran thin with those who drove up the hill, honking their horns and complaining of headaches that had plagued them for two days or more, just as we were sitting down to dinner. Then, his temper would flare, but thankfully, his angry tirades were in German, so the infirm could not understand a word. Sometimes, if I recognized the car in our driveway, I would race down the stairs and whisper to the person holding their head,

'Don't say that you've had the headache for two days!'

'Why not?' they would ask, bleary-eyed. 'Then Doc will think I've been suffering for a long time, and he won't mind me bothering him.'

'No! He'll just think you're silly for showing up now, at dinner, and not at his office earlier during the day!'

'Oh! I understand. Thanks for the hint.'

On the other hand, Doc never complained about having to visit someone who was dying. His compassion for human suffering ran deep, and his personal Hippocratic Oath to make transitions as comfortable as possible, was held close to his heart. Watching him work, I learned a great deal about life and death. Perhaps my only regret in this life is the fact that I did not follow in his footsteps, and become a doctor too.

Remembering times I was in his presence as he worked, I recall two instances which had a tremendous impact on my life and views on dying. For human beings, the question of death is a gripping one—what is death? Why does it happen? As a child, I grappled with these thoughts, trying to fathom the inexplicable. I read books beyond my years, like *The Holy Bible* and *The Tibetan Book of the Dead*, searching for answers. Some innate part of me recognized, even at a tender age, that the physical body is infused with something greater, something alive yet invisible. I wanted to believe that death was not the end, but simply a shift from one realm to another. Most likely, these reflections are what ultimately led me to become a healer, someone who walks the threshold between the physical and spiritual worlds.

One day when I was ten years old, I happened to be in my father's medical clinic, helping him count out tablets. I loved this task because I could be in the same room with him, listening

and learning as he talked to patients about their various ailments. Usually, the waiting room outside was packed with sixty or seventy sick people, some of whom had journeyed for hours from settlements in the north, like Crown Haven or small villages in the south, like Sandy Point. I felt accomplished that day, because he had shown me how to insert a sheet of x-ray film into the large, black metal casing, a job which had to be completed in total darkness, so that the film would not be exposed. As I exited the small dark room holding the cold casing in my arms, I heard loud banging on the side door. Someone was shouting,

'Doc! Open the door! Help me, Doc! My boy is dying! Oh Jesus! My boy is dying!'

My father flung open the door, and a man rushed in holding a young boy in his arms, followed by a woman whom I recognized as my close friend's older sister. The child was quickly placed on the operating table, which stood in the middle of the floor. The tension and dread running through that room were palpable. It is an unforgettable sensation, this standing on the brink of death, mutely witnessing the outcome. The child's little face was streaked in deathly blues and grays, and from the man's panicked words, I gathered that his son had been standing close to a gasoline truck, inhaling the poisonous fumes. Overcome by the deadly toxins, the child had toppled forward, his face near the gasoline. No one had seen him fall.

As the man spoke, my father worked in silence, his arms pumping the tiny chest, his lips trying to breathe life into the slack body. Time stood still. Right then, I saw how untimely death can be, and yet, how timeless its presence remains in our lives. I don't know how long I stood watching, locked between the two worlds of existence, but at some point, my father stopped.

Anxiously I whispered,

'Papi, don't stop! If you keep working, you can still save him!'

While he worked, I felt there was still hope; but I knew that if he stopped, death would have won. That terrified me. It left me trembling and enormously empty. I was afraid to see one so young, so innocent, pass through death's door.

My father stood up, gathering the lifeless body in his arms. I looked into his eyes, deathly serious, the pupils contracted by the gravity of the words he was about to deliver. There was no blood, only the faint smell of invisible gas permeating the air.

Looking directly at the mother, he said,

'Molly, my darling, I am so sorry. There is nothing more I can do. He's gone.'

Molly's mouth opened. At first there was no sound, only the silence in that grief-stricken space, when the world stops turning. Then, a scream; a scream so primal, that my hair stood on end. It is a sound I shall never forget; one of infinite anguish. The piercing cry of every mother who knows this loss. Overcome by a feeling of utter helplessness, I wept too, knowing that nothing could ever fill the abyss of her pain.

A profound silence stayed with me for days. I felt both awed and frightened by the face of death. I struggled inwardly with the overwhelming images I had witnessed, and was struck by the monumental fact that I, too, would die. I wondered how my death would occur. What part of me, if any, would survive this dissolution of the body? Where would I go when my breathing stopped? How was I to live, so that I could die fearlessly? I took to climbing up the high wall beside the house, and sitting with the tiny sugar ants, yellowbirds and passion flowers, I gazed out over the ocean, trying to ascertain what life was about, contemplating my many questions.

My father must have noticed the change in me, and some time later he asked me to accompany him on a house call. I loved going with him in the old Mercedes which smelled of leather, and seeing his worn medical satchel in its place of honour on the back seat. I thought it was a clever case, the way it opened up, the two sides folding out, the little compartments filled with injections, vials, pills, a stethoscope, tourniquets, bandages, and whatever else he needed. I felt important when he allowed me to carry it.

Driving along Bay Street near the sea, he spoke softly.

'I see that you have been troubled by the death of Molly's boy. To witness someone young taken so abruptly is very hard. Even for me, as a doctor who deals with such things, I find myself asking the eternal question, why? I have no answers for you. Only to say that birth and death are part of life. But today I want to show you that death has other ways of taking us.'

'Who are we going to see?' I asked nervously, not wanting to see anyone else die.

'Everything will be all right.' he said reassuringly. 'Just come with me.'

We climbed out of the car. I clutched the medicine bag, the weight of it giving me a sense of security. Whatever my father needed to save someone would be in this satchel. Slowly, we mounted the smooth clean steps leading to the front door of an old wooden house. The bright yellow paint was cracked where the sun and tropical winds had ravaged the walls, but in the garden, red hibiscus and angel trumpets bloomed triumphantly.

'Mrs Archer lives here,' Doc said quietly, as he walked into the house, and steered me past several women respectfully

praying outside the door of a dimly lit bedroom. Inside, when my eyes became accustomed to the darkness, I could see the thin body of a black Bahamian woman curled up on a large bed. Her rich dark hair, laced with gray, fanned the pillow. Her eyes fluttered open immediately, as though she had been waiting for my father. Then looking over at me, she smiled and beckoned me to sit beside her.

'Dis your daughter, Doc?' she asked weakly. 'I is so glad I get to meet her before I go. Listen,' she said in a whisper, so that I had to lean forward to hear her, 'your Daddy done so much good for me, so much good for de people in Abaco. He stayed wid my husband when he die, he bring all my gran'children into dis world, and I done tell him before I leave dis world, I want to see him one mo' time.'

Turning to my father, a slow smile lit up her sunken cheeks.

'Doc, I done told you I want you to hold my hand when I cross over.'

Some images remain imprinted in our minds as beautiful photographs. That day, when my father's strong white fingers grasped Mrs Archer's wrinkled brown hand, I knew the communion that can happen in death between all people, regardless of colour, creed, age or anything else. The sacred bond between us all is our humanity. From behind eyes as deep as wells, she murmured,

'Doc, I is so happy to be goin' home. I want to see my loved ones, all dem who gone before me. I know dey is waitin' for my chariot. And, when I see my sweet Jesus I goin' tell Him about de good doctor in Abaco. But I sure he already know who you is.'

Placing her other hand on a worn Bible beside her, she softly echoed the verse,

'I am the resurrection and the life. He that believeth in me though he were dead, yet shall he live. And whosoever liveth and believeth in me, shall never die.'

With that, her voice faded into nothing, and she took one last breath, as though she were inhaling all the sweet memories of her time on earth, carrying them with her forever, on infinite wings made of air. The only sound remaining was the gentle wailing of the women holding vigil outside her door, mourning the loss of their mother, sister, friend; all the while trusting that their songs of separation and love would be the chorus lifting her onwards, on this part of her journey.

I left that house with the gift of grace. I knew that I had been granted a direct experience of peaceful surrender into something far beyond my childish imagination. In that room, with my father and that old dying woman, I saw that death can also be a letting go, an opportunity for liberation from that which we so firmly grasp in this world. Briefly, I glimpsed the possibility of a luminous union with God, whatever that vastness is, and I felt endowed with a certainty that there is no such thing as nothingness.

Sand In My Shoes

Funerals Are for Singing

There are certain experiences in one's life that are unforgettable. My mother's funeral was one of these. My mother passed away in July. On the day she unexpectedly died, I was in Boston at a healing seminar, which was to change my life forever. Strange, how life and death are so deeply entwined. As she was dropping back into the ocean of oblivion, I was moving forward, taking huge strides into a more conscious life.

I left the seminar early because of her death, and managed to find a flight into Ft. Lauderdale. I was devastated. My mother and I had a rare closeness, very emotional, and at the same time very loving. For all the times she was critical of me, she was also just as supportive, and as I grew older, I began to see that I was actually the stronger of the two of us. She always appeared tough and vivacious to the outside world, powerful and uninhibited, yet I knew the side of her that was fragile, diffident and insecure. I had been there to see her bloom when she became the centre of attention in a group, telling her fabulous stories about a life filled with adventure and love, but I had also been there holding her hand when

cancer left her body weak and diminished. Human beings are so complex, and my mother was no exception.

I arrived in Ft. Lauderdale in a daze. It was all I could do to contain myself, and not start crying hysterically. Standing in the aisle just before disembarking, I thought I would lose my mind and start wailing like a bereaved native woman. I was taut with grief and shock. The hours of having to sit quietly in an airplane with nothing to do but stare out at the empty horizon had driven me to despair. I felt utterly bereft. Never again would I feel her warm hand holding mine. Never again would her sharp voice drive me to the edge of full-blown fury, and never again would her infectious laughter be a balm to my spirit. What a piece of work is man! So filled with contradictions.

I will never forget my gratitude, as I stepped off that airplane and was met by the smiling face of Capt John Roberts, a family friend, who owned his own Cessna. John had come to fetch me and fly me to Marsh Harbour. I do not think I could have stood in one more line, or talked to one more ticket agent. John took my arm, and without many words, drove me to the smaller airport on Perimeter Road, where he bundled me into his small plane and took off.

We flew over the island of Abaco, and when I looked out to see my childhood stretched before me in luscious greens and turquoise blues, I cried, deep sobs wrenching their way out of my heart. There in the distance, on a high hill overlooking the sea, was my home, the place that held so much laughter and so many tears. Capt John said nothing. He knew the intimate nature of death, and how useless words can be in given moments, but in his eyes, I saw both kindness and space.

We landed, the little plane bumping up and down on the uneven runway of Marsh Harbour International Airport.

Seeing the faded pink building, run down by the relentless sun and many travellers passing through over the years, I recalled the last time I saw my mother. I was holding my little boy, and when she hugged us to say goodbye, I was horrified at the words that tumbled out of my mouth.

'Mummy,' I cried, 'this is the last time I'll ever see you alive!'

She drew back in surprise, and so did I. Those words had come out of nowhere.

'What makes you say that?' she asked curious.

'I don't know,' I replied, trying to think of something to cover up my blatant, inadvertent honesty.

She stood there, and suddenly I wanted to clasp her in my arms because she looked so frail, so sad. Her gaze lingered on her grandson, drinking in his essence. His hand reached out to touch her face, and she pressed her cheek into his tiny palm, closing her eyes as though, with that gesture, she could remember the imprint forever. When she looked at me, there was an ageless clarity in her eyes.

'Have we left anything unsaid?' she asked in her straight-forward manner.

'No,' I whispered, 'I just want to tell you again how much I love you.'

We said goodbye and she turned away, climbing into that old white Ford which she often cursed, because unlike my father's fancy Mercedes, it had no power steering. Then, she drove away, waving a wet wipe out of the window.

***

I stepped out of the Cessna onto the tarmac, my reverie broken by the many people waiting to greet me and hold me. They were all crying too. The people of Marsh Harbour loved my mother. They were the first to admit that she could

swear like a man, and if wronged, she would not swallow her anger like a lady. Her retribution was swift and honest, but the people also knew that she was the one to catch their babies in the throes of labour. She was the one who soothed their sweating brows when they were in pain.

They recognized, each in their own way, that with her passing, an era had come to an end. They knew, too, that Doc would not last long without her. I could see the fear in their eyes, because for so many years both my parents had been a reliable source of medical and emotional support. A cornerstone in the community was crumbling.

We drove to the small chapel where the service was to be held. My mother had left explicit instructions that she was to be buried immediately. She did not wish to let her body begin its disintegration in the sweltering heat, under the scrutiny of the people she loved, or disliked, for that matter. My father kept his promise, and with the help of my sister-in-law, Mary, they managed to arrange my mother's funeral for the day following her passing. I have no idea how Mary did this. She arranged the flowers and the sermon. She chose the right hymns, and wrote a eulogy, which is not an easy thing for a daughter-in-law. Mary knew just what to do. I have put it down to the fact that she is Irish, and very organized when it comes to dying.

The little church was crowded, so crowded in fact, that several hundred people stood outside trying to peer in through the slatted windows. There were people from all the settlements in Abaco. They had come from as far north as Fox Town and Cooperstown, while others had made their way from the southern parts like Sandy Point and Cherokee Sound. I wondered how everyone knew, but then in The Bahamas news travels with the speed of light. A silent drumbeat seems

to quiver across the shores, carrying important information.

Everyone moved aside when I arrived. I could hear them whispering,

'Oh Lord! Dat child look jus like her Ma. Oh, an' I know dey was so close. Nurse Gottlieb always tell me how much she love she daughter.'

I moved in a dreamlike state. When grief strikes, it does strange things to the body and the mind. Everything felt unreal. Ninety-five degrees of heat and rivulets of sweat pouring between my breasts did nothing to moisten my mechanical movements. I was suddenly afraid that I might overact when I saw her body laid out in that wooden coffin; all that white satin cushioning her in a cloud. And she never liked satin.

'Too slippery.' she said.

Green moss or palm fronds would have been her choice.

I stumbled up to the altar. There she was. Mary had dressed her in black silk pants and her favourite T-shirt, the one with the tiger sporting emerald green eyes and sequins. She loved sequins. For a woman from such a cultured background, I was always amazed at her love for sparkly things. Another woman would have wanted to go underground wearing elegant Gucci clothes, but not my mother. She liked hot pink and glitter.

I knelt down beside her coffin, awed by the peace on her face. All the wrinkles she so objected to over the years had been smoothed away in death. She seemed to abide in effortless stillness. My lips went to her forehead. Her skin was so cold. Until this day, the memory of that final kiss has remained sealed on my lips. I think it was that very iciness which brought home the fact that she no longer lived in her body.

Behind me, in the front pew, I could hear my father crying,

sucking in his breath in an attempt to quiet the sobs. Someone helped me up and led me to sit beside him. He put his arm around me and I leaned back, closing my eyes.

My mother had always said that she would return from the dead if a woman, whom I shall call Mrs Jay, were to sing at her funeral. I cannot count the times she imitated Mrs Jay's howl, only to fall about laughing at her own singular inability to hold a tune. Having gone to many funerals herself, my mother was well acquainted with the high pitched squawk that so unabashedly emanated from Mrs Jay's throat. Mrs Jay, as I fondly called her, was a pale, somewhat rotund Bahamian lady, a direct descendant of one of the Loyalist families who once graced the Abaconian shores with their presence, and she was ever so proud of that fact.

Aside from this, she was also extremely proud of her singing voice. Over the years, this voice had become notoriously famous for bellowing out *Amazing Grace* or *There's a Cross upon the Hill* in tones that were always slightly off key and distinctly higher than those emitted by the rest of the congregational chorus. That day was no exception. As soon as the organist struck up the chords for the seemingly favourite hymn of the dead, *Abide With Me*, a piercing bawl rent the solemn air. My swollen eyes flew open. I looked at my mother lying so peacefully in her final resting space, and for one incredulous moment, I actually thought that Mrs Jay's voice might bring her back to life. Perhaps she would turn her head and open her eyes once more. Next to me, my father's large frame began shaking. I could feel his shoulders heaving. Concerned, I turned to look at him. His head was bowed, as he fumbled wildly for a handkerchief he hoped was hiding deep in his pocket. Panic-stricken, I realized that my father was not crying,

but bursting with uncontrollable laughter. Many of us know the feeling of deep grief when it verges on hysteria. One sound, one image flashing through our mind, can send us reeling over a giddy edge, and my father had stepped into that precipice. His grief was deep, he was heart broken, I know, but at the same time, Mrs Jay's voice had pushed an irreversible release button. I froze, because I, too, could feel the wild unstoppable giggle rising up from the depths of my belly as her shrill voice sang out the words,

'When other helpers fail and comforts flee,
Help of the helpless, O abide with me.'

We were helpless indeed! It was awful because everyone was looking at us. Father and daughter. How could we possibly be laughing in the face of such inconsolable grief? I have no answer, and I have often wondered why laughter and tears lie so close together. Soon we were both in fits of laughter, trying desperately to retain some semblance of mourning, while the incongruity of it all just extracted further peals from within. Hastily, I grabbed two Kleenex from my purse and shoved them in front of both our faces. Gratefully, the sobbing guffaws were muffled. Safe behind the veil of tissue, we both coughed up memories urged on by the pastoral dirge. I thanked God for tissue that day. Behind us, there were those who saw our heaving shoulders, and I could hear whispering,

'Lord, Doc and his daughter must be takin' dis really hard!'

The truth is, her death was excruciating for me. I was utterly bereft, and my laughter at her funeral was never born out of disrespect. On the contrary, it was filled with loving memories of her. Every fervent note that Mrs Jay sang was meant to lift my mother's soul closer to God. Whenever a verse ended, I thought,

'Now I can breathe without making noise.'

But as soon as the next verse began, I found myself dissolving in laughter once more. In my mind's eye, I saw her laughing heartily as well. Perhaps that was her way of letting me know that she was still present and right there beside us, in spirit, splitting her own imperishable sides at the sound of Mrs Jay's pious chant, and wishing us 'Auf Wiedersehen' when the pastor spoke his final benediction.

Sand In My Shoes

The Soul Snatcher

When I was a teenager, I had a cowboy girlfriend named Trixie Pritchard. She was lean and mean, while I was plump and timid. I both admired and feared her. When she sat on her wild, native stallion, she appeared erect and proud, looking down on the village boys with disdain. My seat in the saddle was far less elegant, and I dreamed that someone would notice me. Some knight in shining white armour. Alas! Most of the boys were pimply-looking individuals who thought it was the height of manliness to drink beer out of bottles hidden in brown paper bags. I trembled in fear before we galloped across a long stretch of beach, whereas she quivered with anticipation to feel the sand stinging her face as it flew off the hooves of her steed. She swore like a man, the 'F word' an integral part of her vocabulary. I giggled nervously when I used the word 'shit.' (A particular shyness, which has long since disappeared.)

Trixie adored her father, Nathan. Nathan Pritchard was a doctor, but he was everything to his daughter: teacher, adventurer, scientist and friend. Above all, he understood her and allowed her wild spirit the freedom it so desperately needed.

I distinctly remember the emergency phone call my father received one night urging him to come to the Pritchard's home. On this evening, Nathan lay dying, the walls of his heart cracking under the strain of a massive heart attack. My father jumped into his car and raced to his friend's side, but death never falters once it has chosen. Nathan Pritchard died with my father holding him.

Now anyone who is familiar with The Bahamas knows that there are churches on every corner, and probably just as many liquor stores. At that time, a minister called Rev Nabb, ran one of these churches. My father, blasphemous as he was, nicknamed him 'The Soul Snatcher' because whenever anyone was dying, the good reverend would appear, slinking behind doors, eagerly awaiting the failing person's end, while simultaneously attempting to convert them into a born-again Christian. He must have had a list of souls that were needed to fulfill his quota. It did not matter to him if many of those he attempted to save from hell were Haitians, and unable to understand a word he was saying, as long as they said, 'Yes' to the question, 'Do you want to be saved?'

Dr Pritchard must have seemed a particularly well-respected catch for God.

My father always said to us, 'If you let Rev Nabb come to my house when I am in the last throes of living, I will surely haunt you after I'm dead.'

Often, when he sat with a dying patient, he would rise and stick his head out of the door, hissing at the minister to go to hell, so great was his distaste for false piety.

That night, the reverend stayed well out of my father's way. I understand he was in the living room persuading Trixie's deaf mother to have the funeral service at his church. Not hearing a word, Mrs Pritchard probably said yes. Armed with

that single word of consent, he left.

A few days later, we all drove down to the bright green church on the dusty road behind the gas station, and somberly entered the packed room. It was one of those hot Bahamian days when the sweat stealthily trickles into any hidden fold of flesh, and the feeling of hysterical claustrophobia is heightened by stale air and too many people.

Trixie sat in the front pew, her spine stoically straight, while Mrs Pritchard wailed in high-pitched tones. I could sense Trixie's impatience with her mother, and this outward expression of grief. Every so often, she would lean into her mother's face and mouth the words, 'Hush Momma!' but Mrs Pritchard refused to take heed. This was her sad moment of tragic glory.

My friend, Trixie, was imbued with a strong sense of justice, and she despised anything that distorted the truth. She knew that her father would not want loud, ostentatious wailing, or fierce preaching of any kind. So, when Rev Nabb climbed up to the pulpit and began to deliver his sermon, I could see the muscles of her slim neck twitching.

He began to talk about how well respected Dr Pritchard was, so far so good. Then he began to say how God always worked His miracles through the doctor ... more neck muscles twitching ... Finally, he launched his holy attack meant to bring all the stray sheep back into the folds of Christianity. Sweating profusely, he bellowed at us mere mortals below, and in that rambling voice that preachers possess, he exclaimed,

'I was with Nathan Pritchard just before he breathed his last.'

(At this point, one could hear members of the congregation saying, 'Thank you, Jesus!')

'And just before he crossed over, I asked him if he wanted

to be saved and born again in Jesus.'

(Here a loud, 'Praise the Lord!')

'And the good doctor cried out to me saying, "Yes, I am ready!".'

(A crescendo of excited 'Hallelujahs' now rising from the mesmerized audience.)

'So you see, even the good doctor turned to the Lord in his final hour!'

Suddenly, there was silence in the church as Trixie rose from where she was sitting. For Rev Nabb, this was a crucial moment because he felt sure that the grieving daughter was stepping forward in miraculous acceptance of Christ.

I watched her stand proud. Rev Nabb was smiling benevolently, encouraging her to come forward with her testimonial, but Trixie wasn't looking for encouragement. She was exploding inside.

'That's a damn lie!' she cried.

(Well honestly, to this day, Trixie and I don't agree on what words were actually spoken. I believe she might have used more emphatic language, but I was sliding under the pew in sheer mortification, so I can't be sure!)

'My father was never a born-again Christian,' she exclaimed boldly, 'and he sure as hell wouldn't want anybody calling him one now! He was a man of truth and he should die with truth!'

Sharp intakes of breath could be heard throughout the pews. I turned to look at my father. Even his face was frozen in surprise, but that did not last long because his ever present sense of humour took over, and he began to laugh so hard that my mother pinched his backside to make him stop.

'Oh! If only my friend, Nathan, could be here! He would

be so proud of her,' he whispered over my head.

The rest of the service remains a blur, but I do remember that as we exited and my father came face to face with Rev Nabb, he looked at the man of God and said,

'Reverend, you know I don't go to many funerals, but I must thank you, for this was undoubtedly the most sincere service I have ever attended!'

Obviously, for weeks after, Trixie was the talk of the town. Some members of the community felt that she was on the sure road to hell. As for me, I was simply in greater awe of her courage.

Grave Laughter

My mother has been dead for many years now, but certain memories still make me laugh out loud—like the day she went to purchase her grave.

Anyone who lives in The Bahamas knows that graveyards in this country are not the epitome of manicured lawns and flowering rose bushes, shaded by large oak trees. Graveyards in The Bahamas are really rather forlorn and sad looking. Slabs of gray concrete, haphazardly placed, create the impression of forgotten tombs, often decorated with faded, plastic flowers of every fake-form and colour. The indestructible wreaths, blown here and there by winds and rain, are often strewn about the dry grass, ending up on headstones for which they were never intended.

My mother used to say that she was quite at ease with this form of graveyard etiquette, because if the living did not give much thought to the dead, then the departed souls were left in peace.

'Let the dead be dead, and the living move on.' she would say. She was ever so practical.

Arising one morning with an irrevocable sense of purpose, which always strengthened during the night and was something to be feared in the morning, she insisted that this was the day she would purchase her final resting place. She was not ill or feeble. Nevertheless, she was determined, and when my mother had set her mind to something, she did not rest until the quest was over.

Applying her Hot Pink Revlon lipstick and spraying herself with Fidgi perfume, she was ready to seize the day.

'Let's go!' she commanded, as she jumped behind the wheel of her Ford pickup truck, hastily stuffing hundred dollar bills into her purse. Never once did I see her sign a cheque, even though she had full access to my father's cheque-books. She was shy about spending money on herself, and always asked my father for hard cash. Cheques made her uncomfortable. When she spent hard cash, she knew exactly where the money went.

Concerned, I asked, 'Are you going to pay for your grave now?'

'Of course!' she answered matter-of-factly. 'What's done is done!'

Down the hill we rattled, over the road she herself had built with two Haitian men. As we passed one of them, she stopped to give him instructions for the day, making sure he would gather all the ripe mangoes and bananas, and fertilize the fruit trees with seaweed and chicken manure.

'Get started,' she ordered, 'I'll help you with the chicken shit when I come back.'

And by God, she was not joking. I cannot recall how often I saw her in that steamy garden, pulling up weeds, digging holes for coconut trees, with sweat pouring off her brow, standing in a torn t-shirt that barely covered her backside. I

would look at her and say,

'Mummy, are these the clothes you wear while working with Johnny?'

'Ja!' she would answer in her thick German accent. 'It's too hot to wear anything else, and he's seen me in a bathing suit before. What's the difference?'

And I suppose she was right. There really was no difference. She was the queen of practicality.

The graveyard manager was waiting for us when we pulled up. Dour-faced and grumpy, he muttered an unfriendly hello and proceeded to lead us through the fenced-in grounds. He was a pallid man; a real Conchy Joe of Royalist descent, with thinning hair, a hook nose, and owlishly thick glasses. A religious man, he preached in one of Marsh Harbour's exclusive churches. So exclusive, in fact, that my mother often said,

'I think Jesus Himself would have trouble getting into that church!'

But she chatted cheerfully, even daring to suggest that a mango tree might do well in the centre of the solemn square.

'Then the children who pass by here after school can enjoy the mangoes, and others who come to commune with the dead will find shade.'

'We don't need any children in here! They just make a mess.' he scowled.

Looking around, I did not see how anyone could make a mess of that sorry plot of land, but I just nodded.

'Isn't this your wife's grave?' asked my mother, pointing to a lonely headstone. 'I'm sure you must miss her. She was a good woman.'

The graveyard manager just grunted.

Whispering, my mother turned to me and winked,
'I might have departed early too, if I'd been married to him!'
We paused at the south side of the rocky field. My mother
squinted her eyes, and looked up toward the hill on her right.

'This is it, sir,' she said. 'This is where I want to be buried.
From here, my spirit can look up and see the house Doc and
I built.'

The graveyard manager nodded and thought for a moment.

'Well, Mrs Gottlieb,' he said in a very business like manner,
'you have two choices. You can either buy two small plots; one
for you and one for Dr Gottlieb, so that when you're both
dead, you can lie next to each other; or if you want to save
money, you can buy one plot of land and dig a deep grave.
You know, like two for one! That way, if you die first, you lie
underneath Dr Gottlieb and if you die after him, you lie on
top of him.'

'Jesus Christ, man!' she exclaimed loudly, her profanity
shocking the good Christian, 'I don't want that! All my life I
had to lie under him or on top of him. I sure as hell don't want
to do it when I'm dead!'

Well, even the graveyard manager could not stop those
thin lips from quivering into a slight smile, while my mother
and I collapsed in fits of laughter. It was so typical of her to
say just what she was thinking. Abruptly, she looked away,
rummaging through her bag to find the money.

'How much?' she asked, trying to control herself.

'Well, for two graves, the cost is five hundred dollars each,
but if you want a deal, the double-decker only costs… '

'No! No!' she cried interrupting him. 'Forget the double-
decker!' Handing him a thousand dollars she smiled, 'Two
graves will do just fine!'

The Snow Owl

One night, shortly after my mother's passing, I was driving along the bumpy road in Smith Point, Grand Bahama—you know, the road right by the sea where one pothole after another keeps your backside fervently bouncing up and down.

It was a cool evening—stars were trailing their light in the black sky. I had just come from visiting a friend when I decided to drive by my parent's old house; the first house they built some fifty years ago. Shoving an old tape into the cassette player, I started humming the strains of *La Paloma*. La Paloma means 'dove' in Spanish, and for some reason my mother adored that song. When her idol, Elvis Presley, recorded it in English, she would play it over and over again.

No more, do I see the starlight caress your hair,
No more see the love-light making your dark eyes shine.

She loved music, especially Elvis.

Anyway, there I was alone in the night, the words *'no more'*

wandering through my heart like a solitary bird, while fresh grief poured over my cheeks. I missed her; the way she made me laugh, the way she could create instant tension with one stern look, and the pure will of her, when she wanted to get things done. But there was a gentleness in her too, something childlike, innocent, fragile.

I drove on, reminiscing, when suddenly out of the darkness, a white, heart shaped face appeared before me, swooping down, golden eyes searching for mine. A strange hooting sound bounced off my windshield. I stopped, shocked! Did I really see that or was it merely my imagination? No! There, flying up through the casuarina trees, was a glistening white snow owl, her wings spanning the width of the circular moon.

'Mummy,' I whispered, an eerie feeling chilling my bones. 'I always wanted you to give me a sign after you died. It is said that the dead speak through our winged friends. Have you come to bring me a message from the other side?'

As I stood there in the night, I remembered that, years ago, she had found an injured snow owl and brought it home, holding it gently in her weathered hands, her red ruby ring sparkling against its feathers. She had been unable to contain her excitement at seeing such a rare bird in The Bahamas.

'These are northern birds,' she said. 'They don't belong here.'

Watching the owl disappear into the night, I wondered where my mother was now. I prayed that she had found her special place in the spirit world, amongst the birds and plants and creatures she so loved. She was so knowledgeable about birds—every species, from swans swimming in the heart of East Prussia, to parrots nesting in the hard limestone of our Bahamian earth. She treasured the little mice that hid in the silver birches in Europe, as much as the soaring frigate birds that follow schools of tuna in the Atlantic Ocean. There was not one creature that escaped her interest, not one flower she could not recognize. I wish I knew as much as she did, but when we are young, we are not interested in these things, and knowledge seems to fade with the passing of our loved ones— carried on the wings of angels to the other side. And then, sadly, it is too late to ask.

Sand in my Shoes

One evening as we sat drinking Chardonnay beneath a tangerine sky filled with sun kissed swallows, I asked my parents this question,

'If you should die before I do, and if there is life after death, will you please give me a sign? I've been reading many books on the subject, but I want tangible proof.'

My father, who was scientifically inclined, just smiled and raised his eyebrows, an indication that I should pursue a more serious line of study. Nevertheless, a few moments later, he looked up from his medical journal and said,

'You know I don't believe in that mystical nonsense, but if there is a way to let you know that a part of me continues, I promise to make myself known from the other side.'

My mother, who was furrowing through our German Shepherd's thick coat, searching for ticks with a rusty pair of tweezers, responded emphatically,

'Well, I do believe in what your father calls that mystical nonsense, and I can assure you that I will give you a sign as soon as I can.'

Then, plucking out another tick, she dropped the bloated blood-sucker into a mug of boiling water where it soon died. Secretly, I feared nothing more than an accidental sip of that vile tick tea in the dark, so I always made certain that the mug was emptied. I imagined those plump gray mini monsters lining my stomach, and sending me a fervent message of retribution.

***

My mother was the first to go, passing from this life as spontaneously as she had lived it. We held an intimate ceremony for her at the beach among the many tall coconut trees she herself had planted. I gathered lush green banana leaves, and placed them on a makeshift altar made of driftwood worn smooth by the waves. The many fruits of her garden—limes, avocados, sugar bananas, mangoes, guavas and sea grape clusters—served as colourful decorations for this farewell party. They were a delicious reminder that, although her body was decaying, her soul lived on in nature.

The final words of wisdom that prepared her spirit to cross the invisible ocean were spoken by her close friend, Michael, a gay Anglican priest who had left the confined thinking of the church, and whose soul mate was a hilarious bar manager. Michael was kind and non-judgemental, and my mother swore that he was a true man of God. She never cared too much about society's rules.

Mother was not a normal woman. Her life was filled with extraordinary acts. She had escaped Germany by jumping into the rushing Rhine and swimming to freedom. She knew how to shoe a horse, stitch a bleeding wound and curse like a soldier. I had even seen her throw back her head, and drink an entire bottle of Remy Martin brandy without flinching. Injured sparrows were cradled gently in her hands, but when my brother

fell ill with an obscure malady that kept him throwing up for months, and turned him into a malnourished toddler, she finally became so fed up that she spoon-fed him his own vomit. There were some who thought these measures were drastic and cruel, but she just shrugged her shoulders.

'Think what you like,' she said. 'I'm his mother and I know what's best for him.'

Although I can't say that I agree with her radical child rearing tactics, the vomiting stopped. Today my brother is a handsome and strapping man. She was a unique character, and so in this last ritual, we raised our glasses and said goodbye to her special way of living.

It was one of those hot steaming evenings in mid July when not one breath of air stirs the leaves, and even the pigeons, weighted by the heavy heat, cease their cooing. As we climbed the hill and headed back to the house, each of us reflected on our personal connection to this eccentric matriarch we called Mummy, this woman whose energetic drive and compulsive need to accomplish things in life could leave the best of us panting in the dust. She had been a breathing monument to the opposing forces that run through people, lashing out at real and perceived injustices with an iron fist, and planting seedlings with a tenderness that was so thoughtful it made me cry.

My father led our little procession; his heart so heavy that I thought the weight of it would pull him to the ground. They were indeed different; she was the earth woman, Artemis, instinctual, primal, while he was Dionysus, the ladies' man, seductive, intellectual, a sensual dreamer always ready for a laugh.

Survival had anchored each in the other. They had come through a war together, losing everything that establishes

normal identity in human beings, and managing to build a life in the tropics, weathering the most primitive conditions, with humour and determination as their only umbrellas. No toilets, no running water, no grocery stores, no cultural events to nourish the mind and relieve the monotonous hum of mosquitoes.

She was a farm girl of high breeding, who learned to deliver babies, staying up night after night with labouring women, so that he could rest and regain his strength for the onslaught of patients who waited outside his clinic every morning. He was a city boy and musician no longer able to visit the opera house. Instead, he became a hunter, spearing lobster and Nassau grouper so they could eat. Their lives were inextricably bound. It made me sad to see his broad shoulders sagging under the burden of loss. She was the hammer and he the anvil but their time of forging was over.

Daughters long to take away the pain, but his was a pain I could not relieve, no matter how unconditional my love. Too many years of intimacy between them, too many chapters not meant for a child's eyes.

We crested the hill, passing through the luxurious gardens she had created, where gardenias generously scented the air with the perfume of heaven, and bright red hibiscus flowers splashed our grieving senses with varying frequencies of exuberant colour. Everything seemed to say,

'Look, I'm here in this corner, under this hedge, beyond that wall! Please don't cry. The rain is water enough!'

Just in front of the entrance to our home stood a Golden Rain Tree. My father admired it, and always told my mother that it was his favourite tree in the whole garden. My mother would laugh and say,

'You love that tree because it's flamboyant and full, just like

a pretty woman!'

And indeed, it was a fantastic tree. Standing proudly against the azure Bahamian sky, it was elegantly vested in many long panicles of bright yellow flowers, which smelled deliciously of lemon mist. The many seedpods it bore were shaped like paper-thin hearts.

I shall never forget what occurred when my father stepped under that flowering tree. As I said before, there was a stagnant lull in the air. Nothing moved. No fleeting breath caressed the boughs. Yet, at the very moment that he stood beneath the foliage, a shower of shimmering blossoms cascaded over him like hundreds of golden raindrops. The petals were everywhere; on his bald head, in his eyes, on his nose and lips, in his hands and clothes and finally forming a beautiful circle of light around his feet.

We stood there, all of us looking on in amazement, while the petals continued to wash over him, like honey clinging to the teardrops on his cheeks and sticking to his tongue, as he opened his mouth to laugh in wonder.

'It's her!' he cried, looking straight at me. 'It's her way of telling us she's still with us!'

We both knew.

***

Years later, I read about the Golden Rain Tree, and found that the flowers are used in China as medicine to soothe the nerves and ease the grieving heart. The tree is named Koelreuteria, after the German botanist who discovered it; a certain Joseph Gottlieb Koelreuter, whose middle name is the same as my father's last name and means "Love of God."

Now, I chuckle when I think of Doc calling the afterlife mystical nonsense.

***

For three years, my mother came to me in dreams, gliding across amethyst shores dressed in flowing robes the colour of purple morning glories. She was never without a blue heron or a white owl. Usually, she brought a message, some words of wisdom to uplift me when my courage dwindled in the mundane world. In these dream spaces, I could talk to her as though she was truly there. We discussed everything from recipes to her new home in the sky.

While she was still alive, guests who came for dinner were often served her incredible Lobster Newburg Bisque. I was disappointed that I had never written down the recipe, and in one of our ethereal conversations, I asked her how she concocted this tasty chowder. She explained every step, and I awoke the following morning with the ingredients clear in my mind.

'It's the sherry that gives it that special flavour,' she smiled. 'If you forget it, you're doomed!'

Our talks were alive and very real, and I felt embraced by her presence. At the risk of sounding slightly schizophrenic, I must confess that I looked forward to my dreams, wondering every night what topics were up for discussion.

Anxious to hear how she passed the time on the other side, I bombarded her with questions.

'It's lovely here,' she would respond. 'I can plant as many mango trees as I like in God's heaven. I simply visualize a tree, and it suddenly appears.'

'Why do you keep coming back?' I asked her, as the smell of her Soir de Paris perfume filled my sleep.

'Oh darling,' she replied, her gaze transfixing me, 'I still have sand in my shoes. I can travel the earth and all the heavens, but that pure lily white Bahamian sand will forever be angel dust

on my feet.' She paused for a moment before adding, 'Your father is preparing to cross his last ocean. I must be on the shore to help him over. After his departure, I won't be visiting you as often. Tell him that I can hardly wait to see him.'

'But he's not even sick!' I burst out.

She nodded faintly. 'I know, but that will not change the way his last chapter has been written.'

'When?' I cried.

As her voice faded, she whispered,

'In one year from now. In the month of June.'

And so it was.

***

My brother climbed the stairs, holding the small wooden box that contained our father's ashes.

'It's hard to believe that a man as big-boned as Doc, and with such a generous sense of humour, now fits into a little box,' he murmured, teary-eyed.

I, too, wondered, 'Where does a life go? In what album are the thousands of memories arranged for safe-keeping?'

At that moment, my five-year old son bounced into the room holding the chain his grandfather had always worn.

'Mommy' he cried, pointing to a tiny silver charm dangling from the necklace, 'Doc said he wanted me to have this. It has the shape of an eye. He told me he would always watch over me, even when he was gone. So, can I have it? Please? Please?'

We pried the charm off the chain, and my son, who was thrilled, went charging down the grassy path toward the beach, clutching the amulet in his chubby hand.

'Be careful!' I shouted 'You don't want to lose it.' But he had vanished.

He soon returned wailing like a banshee, his little face

streaked with dirt and tears.

'It's gone! I dropped it!' he cried in his childish voice. 'There are too many rocks and so much grass! I can't find it. Mommy, you find it!'

There was no use in reprimanding him, or telling him how hopeless I thought my search would be. His boyish heart was already breaking, and so I set off in the scalding mid-day sun, my eyes raking every inch of that rocky road, while my fingers sifted through half a mile of grass and gravel.

After two hours of laborious searching, a feeling of failure set in. Sweat was running in rivers through my hair, and I was exhausted. Turning back, I trudged up the hill. The horseflies were wicked that day, stinging my face and the backs of my legs with rare defiance. As I stopped to slap one away, I felt my frustration rising.

'Doc,' I yelled at the sky, 'you promised that you would give me a sign if there was life after death! Well, it's too damn hot, and this path is too long, and I feel like I'm going to collapse. So, if you're still around, please do me the favour and show me the way! Okay?'

The horsefly fell into the dirt, and as I stooped forward to see if it was truly dead, my eyes fell on the tiny amulet wedged between two stones.

'Oh my God,' I whispered, 'this can't be true!'

But it was true. My fingers trembled as I picked up the object. After so many years of rubbing against Doc's hairy chest, the metal on the eye was worn thin. Now I pressed it to my own heart and looking up, I felt my eyes welling with gratitude. Suddenly, the clear blue sky began to spry tiny drops of sparkling rain. My eyes scanned the heavens, but not one cloud was floating there. This uncanny phenomenon of

rain falling from nowhere is one that has always filled me with wonder, and often incites Bahamians to remark,

'Today must be a good day 'cause de good Lord so happy He is cryin' for joy!'

And I knew how He felt.

Epilogue

Rose

Before me stands a crystal decanter, beveled patterns throwing off a shower of light. One rose. Sunlight filtering through paper-thin petals. Peachy golds, strawberry reds. The slender stem, a fulcrum for the blossoming maze, which opens to revere the sun in spite of being severed from the source that feeds it.

Fragrance wafting across my verandah carried on gentle sea breezes. There must be a word to describe this scent. But I am lost. Every scent is so unique. Other writers know so well the magic of the written word, yet I feel empty in the face of such magnificence. Still I must try.

The scent is sweet, like my favourite Bulgari perfume, yet it does not dull my senses. It rises like an invisible cloud of fresh green tea, titillating me. I want to dive into this fragrant pool, and breathe in until my lungs pop with greedy pleasure.

I wonder if I could write a love letter on these petals. No! It would be a desecration—the hand of man already leaves its mark on every creation of nature. But certainly, if I waited for every petal to fall to the cool tiles, and then pressed them between the

pages of a poetry book, later I could write 'I love you' on each tiny piece of coloured parchment. No, perhaps I'll just eat the petals, or bake a rose cake and gorge on their essence.

I look again, my eye searching for detail, for some small thing to initiate my self-expression. I see veins, tiny orange and yellow veins, emanating molecules of spirit. I long for my heart to open like this rose. Then, my beloved would bow his head toward my breast and breathe in the very soul of me.

Shining valiantly on the eve of life, this rose stands so proudly, swaying to the world's silent melodies; an embodiment of both vulnerability and strength. I wonder ... how will I be when the sun begins to set on my life? Will I burst forth with generosity, gladly giving of myself as I stand dying? Bowing my head, I pray.